The Journey to
Paradise

The Journey to
Paradise

STEPHEN STRIPE

&

KEVIN STRIPE

iUniverse, Inc.
Bloomington

The Journey to Paradise

iUniverse books may be ordered through booksellers or by contacting:

iUniverse
1663 Liberty Drive
Bloomington, IN 47403
www.iuniverse.com
1-800-Authors (1-800-288-4677)

ISBN: 978-1-4620-2671-5 (sc)
ISBN: 978-1-4620-2672-2 (ebk)

Printed in the United States of America

iUniverse rev. date: 06/23/2011

CONTENTS

Introduction vii

Chapter 1 Background and Wish 1

Chapter 2 The Village: Dream or Reality?...................8

Chapter 3 The Raid 14

Chapter 4 Defense..20

Chapter 5 The Road..25

Chapter 6 The City..33

Chapter 7 A Calling, a Business 41

Chapter 8 Expedition 47

Chapter 9 Experiment and Invention 53

Chapter 10 Sermon 58

Chapter 11 Artillery 62

Chapter 12 Opening Shots 64

Chapter 13 Rescue Mission 69

Chapter 14 Captured 72

Chapter 15 Betrayed 75

Chapter 16 The Battle 78

Chapter 17 Victory Celebrations...............................84

Chapter 18 Hospital Salvation 86

Chapter 19 An Evening at Home with Friends...........89

Chapter 20 The Heretic 94

Chapter 21 Trial 99

Chapter 22 Trial Outcome.......................................110

Chapter 23 Escape...114

Chapter 24 Destiny 117

INTRODUCTION

Hypatia was a mathematician, philosopher, astronomer, and teacher who lived during the final days of the Roman Empire in the Greek city of Alexandria. She was reported to be a leader or principal advocate of the neo-Platonic school of philosophy. Although reputed to be of exquisite beauty, she had no interest in marriage. Hypatia was the last scientist associated with the ancient library of Alexandria.

That library contained the knowledge of centuries. Complete works of the Greek philosophers, playwrights, and scientists, along with other ancient manuscripts from all over the world, were stored and studied in that institution. Intellectual development, from Babylonian through Egyptian works and those from the classical period, could be found there. Great discoveries were made or recorded there.

It was a time of great conflict. The Christian Roman emperor Theodosius published an edict prohibiting various aspects of pagan worship. Christians throughout the empire embarked upon a campaign to destroy or Christianize pagan temples and other sites. Hypatia was a pagan and friend of the imperial governor Orestes. The patriarch or bishop of Alexandria was Cyril, who was in conflict with Orestes. Cyril had books revised to reflect Christian dogma. He had great difficulty with Hypatia because she was a scientist and a woman. Science at that time was considered pagan and hence black magic. Women were considered second-class citizens, if not property. The church was dominated by men, and its hierarchy was considered to be the sole domain of men. The proclamations and edicts of the church were to be taken literally. Peter, a charismatic zealot who was a supporter of Orestes, led a mob action. Hypatia was attacked by a mob of fanatical Christians and was stripped and filleted alive with oyster shells. This was the manner in which witches were killed at that time. Some time later, the great library of Alexandria, along with most of the knowledge it contained, was burned to the ground. Very few works have survived to this day. Another version has the library being burned and destroyed at the time of the Muslim conquests, again because it was pagan.

Most of the knowledge of the ancient world was lost for one thousand years; it was called the Dark Ages. It wasn't until the Renaissance, the time of the Enlightenment, when the knowledge—or at least a portion of it—was rediscovered by Copernicus, Galileo, Bruno, Newton, and others. All knowledge during the Dark Ages and Medieval times was suppressed unless it conformed to accepted religious dogma. When it was being rediscovered by the new scientists and thinkers, they were persecuted by the church authorities, and this meant imprisonment or death. Bruno was burned at the stake for heresy; his crime was suggesting that there were other worlds with possible life in the cosmos. Galileo was arrested and tried for heresy for daring to say that not all objects in the universe go around the earth. He championed the idea that the planets, including the earth, go around the sun, as Copernicus had theorized. And this he demonstrated this fact by scientific observation. It was not until the twentieth century that Galileo was pardoned by the church and that his teachings were accepted as true.

What would have been achieved if the world hadn't gone into the Dark Ages?

Are we about to burn down the library again? The conflict and controversy about evolution and the beginning of the universe are only two issues much feared by the religious fundamentalists. This is because it is at odds with their interpretation of scripture. It seems that extremism, religious or otherwise, only appreciates more powerful weapons that can be provided by science. The growing fundamentalism of various religions, Christian and non-Christian, is uncompromising and increasingly litigious and violent. The revolt against scientific enlightenment and the violent, uncompromising religious extremism are connected. This fundamentalism threatens the modern library.

The average person is probably not interested in science beyond the latest appliances or weapons it can provide. He is easily led by charismatic clerics, such as Jim Jones, Osama Bin Laden, Jerry Farwell, the Ayatollah Khomeini, Pat Robertson, and others. This time, however, the weapons are nuclear, chemical, and biological. These weapons will destroy not only the library, but everyone and everything else. The great danger behind fundamentalism is intolerance. The events of 9/11 were due in part to religious fundamentalism. The fundamentalism of competing religions threatens not only science, but our very existence on this planet. The new Dark Age may be one that will never end with a new renaissance. The bishop Cyril, who lived at the time of the destruction of the great library of Alexandria, was later canonized as a saint.

What would it be like to be transported to a religious paradise that suppressed science?

CHAPTER 1

Background and Wish

John and Mark had walked out at the conclusion of a debate between members of the Skeptical Society and those of the religious right. The topic was the science of evolution in relation to Genesis. Big names such as Michael Shermer, Richard Dawkins, Sam Harris, Pat Robertson, Ken Ham and Carl Baugh among others were on stage dueling it out in front of a sold-out audience at the Civic Auditorium in Omaha. The arguments were heated and intense and drew supporters on both sides of the issue. As they left the convention center, both men were quiet and deep in thought.

John Pope, a pastor at a local church, was a few years out of seminary. Mark was working for the same family medicine program where he had completed his medical residency. The two men had been buddies since their years at Hastings College, a church-affiliated, Liberal Arts College. They had often attended college functions and gone on double dates. After they had completed graduate studies, they found it a bit more difficult to get together, so any excuse to see each other—even a heated debate—was good.

They walked in the rain to Mark's car, neither one saying a word. Once they were in the car, Mark finally turned to John and broke the silence. "After that, you want to go get a drink and maybe a bite to eat?"

"Sure, that sounds good." Replied John with a grin.

"I know a good, out-of-the-way place on Saddle Creek Road. Okay with you?"

"Sure, wherever. This weather is atrocious."

"Sure is. What did you think of that . . . the debate?"

John slumped in his seat. "Wow, I don't know yet. I haven't digested it all."

"How are Laura and the kids?"

"Oh, they're fine, thanks. Growing and growing. You know kids. Laura has her activities at the YMCA, the PTA, and all the other alphabet organizations." John laughed. "I wish I had more time to spend with them. The church takes up so much time. Visiting the sick in their homes, hospitals, and nursing homes takes a great amount of time. Our church just started a program to help the homeless. We provide them with meals, find them a place to stay if possible, and have them over for holiday dinners when we can."

Mark was impressed, "You're so lucky to have a family like that. I hope some day I'll find the perfect wife like you did. I can still picture Laura at your wedding. Her long, golden hair and cute looks definitely turned my head. She was absolutely beautiful. You're lucky you didn't miss your own wedding. Being the best man, I would've had to marry her for you if you hadn't shown up, you know. Honor and all that." Mark grinned and added, "John, you have always had an eye for the ladies."

John smiled. "I guess it was a good thing that I made it, eh? Anyway, do you have time as a doctor to find somebody so you can get hitched?"

"I guess I'm not as lucky as you are. I'm busy all the time, practicing medicine and teaching. It's different being the professor rather than a resident. We have a number of foreign medical graduates. We have had Hindus, Buddhists, and Muslims. Sometimes I get into discussions with them about their countries, cultures, and religions. They are all smart and good docs; however, I find it difficult to understand their fervent, unquestioning loyalty to a system of beliefs. Ah, here we are. I'll let you out at the door so you can get us a booth while I park, OK?"

As he entered the Bar and Grill, John removed his trench coat and spied an empty booth in an isolated corner. The waitress indicated for him to follow her as she led him to the booth he'd pointed out.

"Miss, a friend of mine will be joining me shortly," John said. "Could you please show him to the table when he gets here?"

She nodded and asked, "Would you like to order a drink while you wait for your friend?"

"No thanks," John replied, opening the menu. Waiting those few moments allowed the words of the debate to reenter his mind. Just then Mark came in and headed toward him, removing his coat.

Sitting down, Mark commented with a chuckle, "It is really coming down hard out there! Maybe we should start building an ark."

John, laughing too, said, "Yeah, it doesn't need to rain for forty days and forty nights around here. The flooding will start as soon as the sewers begin to back up."

"You were saying something in the car about the foreign graduates' beliefs," John said. "What was it?"

"Yes, some of them adhere to literal interpretations of their Scriptures, even if they can be shown to be false by various means. They all believe to some degree or another their faith is the one true religion."

John leaned back in his chair. "It all depends on what one is brought up on."

At that moment, the waitress returned for their order. Mark spoke first. "Could you bring me a whiskey sour, an order of onion rings, and a bratwurst, please?"

John was looking at the menu and then looked up at the waitress. "One of your charburgers and a beer will do me fine."

As the waitress headed off in the direction of the kitchen, they continued on with their conversation.

"Throughout history, more people have been killed in the name of God than for any other reason," Mark said.

"Do you still go to church?" John said his voice rough.

"No. . . . No, I don't," Mark said, looking down at the table. "Church doesn't seem to provide me with the answers that it once did. Maybe spiritually it did, or does, provide answers, but I've done quite a bit of reading and studying, and I've found many problems with religion . . . any religion. And the extremes lead to violence. Hey, remember back when we were in college and we both had to take religion courses and science courses?"

John nodded.

"I've always been interested in religion," Mark rushed on, "but I find its explanations don't jive with what we really know through science. If religion . . . well, science provides a way of testing reality. And what is worrying me more is the growing conflict between religions, at least the fundamentalist elements of each claiming to be the one, true religion. What does true religion mean?"

At that moment, the waitress placed their orders on the table and left.

John said, "I see your soul is being tortured. But God through Jesus Christ has shown us the way. The Bible is the only true book. It is the word of God. It has shown us the way to salvation."

Mark stopped him. "Wait a minute, just one damn minute. You're saying that Christianity is the only true religion also? Your form of Christianity or somebody else's form?"

"What our prophet, the founder of my church, has shown us is the true way," John said. All others are just shadows or pretenders, or they have lost the calling."

"Your prophet? Your prophet says you have the right way, and nobody else does!" Mark was aghast. He didn't know that John had become such a fervent Christian and, he was afraid, a fundamentalist, too.

John was animated. "Yes, our prophet. He has taught us that the Bible is the source of all knowledge. And all knowledge is from God, through the Scriptures."

"Look," Mark said, "the Roman Emperor Constantine legitimized Christianity and made it the state religion. He codified the books of the Bible under a commission headed by Bishop Eusibius. It was the duty of that commission to decide which of the many books circulating at the time were to be included in the Christian Bible. So if God wrote the Bible, why did a commission of men have to decide which books to include or not include?"

This remark infuriated John, but he knew it was true. He said, "It was God who inspired them to write the holy books. He used men to organize his word and to cull out the false words."

John staring at him thought he had better convert Mark because he could see that Mark's soul was in danger.

Even before this night, John had told Mark over and over, "If you do not accept Jesus Christ as your Lord and savior and the literal word of the Bible as inspired by God, then you would be condemned to hell and damnation." Now John repeated his remark, louder and with more emphasis.

Mark replied excitedly, "Why will I be damned to hell if I do not accept your version of Jesus Christ? And saved from what?"

"Because Jesus said in the Bible in John 14:6 'I am the way.' The Bible is the only truth, and therefore your science is an atheistic interpretation of God's wonders, and it is that from which you must be saved!" said John loudly and with righteous indignation.

Mark argued, trying to tone it down a bit and with logic, "The Bible was written by man and, as such, contains many contradictions. For example, look at the two accounts of the flood. One version in Genesis 7:12 has the flood caused by rain alone, and the rain falls for forty days and nights. Another version in Genesis 7:11 has the windows of the heaven open and the fountains of the deep open up, and it lasts for 150 days."

John responded forcefully, "It did rain for forty days and forty nights, and with underground water springing forth, the flood lasted 150 days. There is a scientist at Los Alamos, what's his name . . . Baum . . . Baumgardner, Dr. Baumgardner has a computer program to prove it. It is the dogma of the branch of science called evolution that is particularly wrong."

Mark sounded furious. "Dogma? You're using a religious term meaning a code of beliefs or body of doctrines proclaimed by a church in describing a branch of science. That's interesting but wrong. It is not beliefs; it is facts. The vast majority of scientists agree with evolution . . . the evidence from fossils, genetics, and geology supports it."

Mark leaned forward toward John holding his brat. "Has anyone ever checked that Los Alamos scientist's program, but him? He is a geologist. And he is a known fundamentalist Christian. I know of him. I admit that while science is not perfect, it does provide a method for explaining the universe, including the big bang and evolution. It is self-correcting discipline. If a natural explanation could be found, why is it necessary to invoke a supernatural one? Remember, extraordinary claims require extraordinary proof. Where is the proof of God and miracles? The scientific method is consistent and follows the same logic from one branch of science to another. Therefore, rejecting evolution would mean rejecting all science. And without science, its child, technology, would not be possible. Therefore, all the modern conveniences and wonders of today would not exist."

John said, "Only evolution is flawed. And the same logic is not used from one branch of science to another. Evolution has become a religion to those that espouse it, and its logic runs counter to the evidence. And where is the extraordinary proof of evolution? Science must be viewed through the lens of scripture."

"Come on, John. Be reasonable. Evolution is not a religion. Those that say it is, like those you were obviously influenced by, use that argument only as a counter to their creationism or intelligent design as a part of their religion. Those that do not are not part of mainstream science, or if they are, they don't speak from a position of expertise on evolution, as it is not in their field of science. They also speak from a position of passion based on their religious beliefs, not logic or science. Where is the proof of creationism or, for that matter, God? Why do I have to accept the literal truth and mysteries of the Bible to be saved? And saved from what? Hell is nothing more than the fantasy of punishment after death to coerce a particular way of thinking! That is only your view and the view of those who would rather accept mythology and fantasy over fact."

In the heat of argument, the volume of their voices was well in excess of the music volume. They were making a scene. John and Mark could not or would not change their minds or compromise.

The waitress came over and asked, "Could you please calm down, or we will be forced to ask you both to leave."

John was boiling but said he was sorry, as did Mark, and both agreed that they would keep the discussion civil.

After calming down, Mark thought about his long friendship with John, a person he really liked. That the friendship might be sacrificed to uncompromising beliefs depressed him. Mark wanted to try finding a ground that was common to both so that their friendship could be preserved.

"I'm sorry," Mark said. "Why can't we discuss these issues in a calm civilized debate and maybe find some common ground to both sides?" But John would hear none of it

They both finished their food in silence. Mark offered to give John a lift back home. John refused, saying, "No, I will not ride in the same vehicle with a non-believer. I'll call a taxi!"

"Come on, John. I am sorry we got into this fight. We should have never gone to that damn debate. It is raining out, and I can take you home. We are still friends, aren't we?"

John turned with fire in his eye. "No I will call a taxi. You need to come to your senses, and Jesus will forgive you. Science is not always right. I wish there wasn't any science or at least the kind that ignores God. If there wasn't any Godless science, then the world would be a better, holier place."

Mark, shocked, said, "No, John you don't mean that about no science." John put on his trench coat went out and hailed a cab, not even looking back at Mark once.

Mark put on his coat, feeling bad, and walked out into the rain and got into his car. He sat there for couple of moments, thinking of what had just transpired, and then shrugged his shoulders, started the car, and left the parking lot. He mumbled to himself as he was driving, "John will come to his senses, and we will be able to talk again. I know that guy."

CHAPTER 2

The Village: Dream or Reality?

When John got home, Laura asked why he'd taken a cab. "Didn't you leave with Mark?" she asked, helping him out of his wet coat. "What happened?"

"Mark is a lost soul." John said, still sounding angry. "We went to a debate, that damn debate! Science always seems to come out on top in such things. Is there no room for faith anymore? Aren't the Scriptures evidence enough of creation and truth?"

Laura said, "I'm sorry. Mark is your best friend. Call him, John. You two have always been able to work things out."

"No, I won't. He has to call me."

"I'm sorry you feel that way, John." She embraced him. With that tenderness, he calmed down. He smiled at her, saying, "I'm sorry, sweetheart. I didn't mean to bring all this home with me."

"That's okay, honey. We'll talk about it later. Are you hungry?"

"No, we stopped and had a bite to eat before all of this happened. Our debate was so hot and furious that we both got caught up in the subject. It made us both forget ourselves. If there was no science without God, then this wouldn't be an issue. I wish there was no Godless science!"

That night as he was going to bed, his wife heard him murmuring this wish, over and over, until he fell asleep.

Later, as consciousness slowly began tearing him away from sleep, John noticed that the bed didn't feel right. The softness of his pillow and mattress was replaced by an uncomfortable stiffness and lumps driving their way into his back and legs. There also seemed to be long, dull-pointed needles covering the entire bed. Lying in bed, confused and feeling a slight chill around his body, John heard the voices of children playing, coming from somewhere outside the house. These sounds struck him as being odd because in the bed, normally, he couldn't even hear cars drive past.

John opened his eyes and waited for the remaining effects of sleep to leave his vision. The plaster ceiling from the night before had been replaced by wooden beams covered by thatched straw. The walls were made of wood and rock with mud used as mortar. Next to him, the space where Laura slept was empty. However, he could hear her conversing with another woman, whose voice he did not recognize. John gave a small laugh as he stood on the cold, hard-packed dirt floor. He must be still dreaming. He hadn't heard the alarm' go off yet.

He stood beside of the bed, inspecting the bareness of the room. The bed lay low to the floor. The covers were made of roughly woven wool cloth. The mattress was a cloth sack stuffed with straw. The room was small, and in one corner was a small bed for children. It reminded him somewhat of a cabin he had been to when he went on school field trips as a child. An ancient-appearing ceramic oil lamp, a clay pot, and a knife were placed on a small wooden table. A bow, several arrows made with iron heads, and a few other items he couldn't recognize were hanging along the wall. The only other thing in the room was a wooden chest. He stepped over to it and pulled open the heavy lid. The chest contained very basic, coarsely woven tunics and trousers of various earth tones.

Behind him came the voice of his wife. "Finally up, I see." John turned around, but it took a minute before he realized it was Laura.

Her hair was darker with a hint of grey; she looked like she had aged ten years. She was wearing a coarsely woven green sack dress tied around the midriff with a cord. Before he could open his mouth, Laura asked, "What is wrong, dear?"

John smiled, "I must still be dreaming."

His wife walked over and pinched him on his right arm. John yelped a little in pain, "Ouch! What was that for?"

She giggled, "Don't you know?" She tilted her head to one side. "If you want to find out if you're dreaming, pinch yourself. Now put your clothes on. The garden needs tending before holy services."

He looked back into the chest and noted that the clothing options were rather limited. He dressed in a plain brown tunic with trousers and found them incredibly itchy. In the corner he found his shoes, which were a pair of leather sandals that laced up. As he sat on the bed to lace up the sandals, he began examining the room again. There was one crude, shuttered window in each of three outside walls of the room. A small, arched doorway was in the fourth inside wall. He wasn't sure of what he was seeing, nor could he believe it.

As he exited the small bedroom doorway, he found himself in a slightly larger room, just as bare but with a central fireplace and a shuttered window in each wall and a door leading to the outside. Staring at him from a stalled space in the opposite corner of the room was a cow. They both stared at each other until the cow lost interest and resumed munching hay from a manger. A couple of sheep occupied the stall with the cow, and they ignored John.

The house smelled of smoke, animals, and other unrecognizable odors. John saw his wife and another woman cooking something in a large iron pot over the fireplace. Cuts of dried meat, sausages, vegetables, cheeses, and other items were tied by rope and string to the large wooden beams in the roof. Along the wall were a chest, clay pots, and some ancient agricultural implements. On a shelf were a stack of neatly folded cloth blankets. Next to the blankets, a well-used sling with a leather pouch hung on the wall.

John exited through the small, open doorway that had a crude wood door attached by bronze hinges. Outside in the bright sunshine, he noticed that there were many small houses similar to the one he had just emerged from. The houses were arranged in a roughly circular pattern around a central village plaza. There was a twelve-foot-high, rough-hewn stone wall surrounding the village, with gates and towers approximately every thirty yards. Each gate was guarded by two men wearing bronze plate armor breastplates with the sign of the cross boldly painted in red. Each man carried a broad-bladed, hilted iron sword in a scabbard at his hip and a spear in his left hand. There was one guard per tower, armed with bow and arrows.

About two dozen children were scattered about the village playing, and two of them resembled his own, Brandon and Cindy. The children ran past him and turned the corner laughing playfully. Everyone was dressed in a mix of animal skins and coarsely woven cloth tunics. The men wore pants and the women wore dresses. The women appeared to be wearing jewelry made of shells, stones, and bronze figurines. Some of the men wore necklaces made of arrowheads or bronze medallions. The children were running around barefoot, while the adults wore leather sandals. Some of the men were carrying a variety of weapons or tools made of wood, iron, or bronze.

Could he be dreaming or hallucinating about being an American Indian or a medieval peasant? John was not quite sure which. This certainly is not the twenty-first century.

He walked to an open gateway and the guard acknowledged his presence with a nod and a smile. John returned the gesture, and proceeded to some high ground just east of the walled village from which to survey the landscape. A high, snow-covered mountain dominated the landscape to the north of the village. The village was situated in a somewhat lush valley basin with a central artesian spring and an accompanying pond. The small pond provided water for the surrounding plants, livestock, and wildlife. The village sat southeast of and bordering the pond. A stream ran from the pond to the southwest. There were trees crowded around the pond and stream with grasses on the periphery. A flock of sheep was being tended by a shepherd in a grassy field. One area of the valley appeared to be cultivated and had irrigation ditches running to it from the spring. What appeared to be a road made of flat stones peaked in the center of the thoroughfare with curb stones on either side entered the valley from northeast, passed through the village walls, and exited through the hills to the southwest side. The hills and the ground around the valley appeared to be semi-arid. He reentered the gate to the village.

On the other side of the plaza was a structure constructed of stone, and it was larger than any of the houses by several times. To John's amazement, it had a cross jutting up from the roof and windows of multicolored glass in the walls. Next to that structure, there was a cemetery with stone markers and a free standing bell tower. Several men were going in and out of the church. One man was dressed in long, white robes. The other two wore course brown robes with hoods. They all had cropped hair of various hues and full beards.

John approached the nearest group of men, who had a somewhat familiar look about them, and asked, "What's going on?"

The younger man said, "Master Pope, we have just returned from a hunting expedition to the wooded plain west of the village. We were successful. The game we got will be divided among the people. However, we met some people who belong to the older religion, so we remained discreet about our interactions with them."

"Why?" John asked.

The oldest of the five men, looking puzzled, asked John, "Don't you remember the time of the great persecution, as told by the elders?"

John thought for a moment, not daring to appear ignorant, and then replied, "Oh, . . . yes, I remember." He thought he should try to look as knowledgeable as possible in this new environment.

The hunters then told their stories of the latest hunting trip to the west. Then they asked if John was going to attend church. John nodded and walked with them to the church on the other side of the plaza. He met Laura and the children at the entrance to the church.

Upon entering the church, he noticed that there were no seats. There was an altar and the familiar podium next to it at the front of the church. The podium had three objects resting on it—a smaller bronze cross, a chalice, and a candlestick. A large bronze cross was mounted on the wall at the front of the church where all could see it.

All the men stood up front close to the altar, while the women and children stayed in the back. The man leading the congregation was referred to as Father Paul. He was wearing a long, white robe with a large bronze cross on a chain about his neck. He was the only one reading from a large, worn, illustrated book on the podium, which appeared to be a Bible. The other men in the brown robes seemed to be assisting Father Paul in the service. Collecting the offerings of money or goods from the worshipers was one of their tasks. They would show individuals to their places for services. The assistants, also, would give anyone encouragement with a rod who didn't show the correct amount of enthusiasm. In the first part of the meeting, Father Paul recited the Nicene Creed, and the congregation followed his recital by saying "Amen." Father Paul started his sermon with a short synopsis of the birth, life, and death of Christ, and stated the subject of the sermon: the resurrection of all those who believe in Christ and the damnation of those who do not. He also spoke of the need to spread the faith to all peoples. John found himself liking this church and this place. At the end of the service, John rushed to Father Paul to express his appreciation for such an insightful and moving sermon.

John left the church with his family, feeling rather good about the village and the church, although he was a little confused on how he got there and what it all meant. He returned to his house, and his wife served the meal of mutton and gruel. After he was served, she served her two children and then herself. The meal was rather bland but wholesome.

John asked Laura, "Who was the woman cooking with you this morning?"

"She is our neighbor, Margaret. You remember, don't you? She's the wife of Aaron. We often cook at each other's houses. You know we share the food between our households . . . you remember?"

John nodded and said, "Oh, yes, I didn't recognize her from the back with that different dress on." Laura looked at him, puzzled, and then continued with her tasks. He then finished his explorations of the village.

The following day, John awoke at sunrise. He got dressed and ate what breakfast he could find, which consisted of a piece of rye bread and some figs. After kissing his wife and hugging his children, John went out into the village to try to learn more about his circumstances. John learned that most of the men in the village were part-time warriors. Some were black smiths who repaired and fashioned new tools or weapons. Most worked the fields and tended the livestock. The women took care of their families, cooking, repairing clothing or making new garments. John found out his main function was to act as school teacher and assistant to the head of the village.

CHAPTER 3

The Raid

John was seated on a rock overlooking the sheep in the field, resting and thinking. A group of about dozen and half men of varying ages, all of them carrying weapons, approached him. When they neared, the youngest of the group asked, "Master Pope, will you accompany us?"

John turned toward him. "To where? To do what?"

The young man stared at him blankly for a moment and then started to answer, but the oldest man pushed him aside and said, "John, we need your help in a raid on that village of non-believers three leagues to the east."

They handed John a spear, a sword in a scabbard on a belt, and a round, wooden shield. John was astonished at the brazen way they approached him to ask his help in an act of violence. But he dared not reveal his thoughts at this point. It would have marked him as different and put him and his family in danger from the other villagers. So he nodded in agreement, and they started walking down a rough path off the main road that was strewn with rocks and boulders. The landscape became increasingly semi-arid and hilly as they progressed.

After about an hour of walking, John asked, "Why are we attacking this village?"

The oldest one, named Stevens, answered. "John, you know this. We need to avenge the deaths of our brothers who were killed by the non believers last winter. Also, we are in need of hostages to gain information on when they're planning to attack our village. Remember last week when some of their slaves escaped and made their way here? Several of the slaves told us that preparations for war were being made. You remember? Anyway, having hostages will give us an edge in possible negotiations. Maybe we can avert or delay the attack."

John replied, "Couldn't we talk to them?"

Stevens stopped in mid-stride, turned around, and replied, "Negotiation without an advantage is useless. You know that, John. Think for a moment. We have been at war with these people off and on for a long time. We cannot even begin to talk unless we have something they want or need. They will not listen." With that, he began walking again.

John was quiet for several minutes as he walked with his comrades. He finally said, "I'm sorry. You're right."

As they progressed toward their target, John was listening very intently to his comrades' chatter. He could make out that the target village followed a newer religion, which did not recognize Christ as the Son of God. Some members of their village were captured by that group and were tortured until they either died or were converted to the new religion. The other village also had a holy book that was said to have been revealed to them by their prophet.

It was about dusk by the time they reached the enemy village. They hid below the crest of a hill, behind some boulders overlooking the enemy village. The village was composed of stone houses arranged in two concentric circles and surrounded by a wall approximately ten feet high with multiple gates. In the middle of the village was their holy structure. At each of its four corners were pillars with a black semicircle atop each. On either side of that holy structure were two larger houses, apparently the homes of two of the most important people in the community, probably the leaders.

It was time for the main raiding party to formulate a plan. Stevens motioned for two of the raiding party to reconnoiter the village. They returned a little while after sunset.

One of the scouts breathlessly and excitedly said, "There is a north gate close to the cover of a riverbank. The trees and shrubs will provide good concealment in approaching that gate and the guards. The south gate is close to the cover of a ravine. The cover isn't so good there, but the boulders and the background of the hills will break up your outlines and make it difficult for the defenders of that gate to identify you before you attack."

Stevens spoke to his second in command. "Phillip, in about one hour, take your section to the ravine and overpower the sentries of the south gate as quietly as possible. Enter and make your way quietly to your target house on the south side of the plaza. I will take a section with John to the river and enter from the north gate. Wait until you see us surround the other target house. We will enter the houses at the same time and capture their leaders. Afterwards, withdraw out of village as expeditiously as possible. We will rendezvous at this spot."

As they lay on the rocky ground, waiting for the hour to pass, John could feel his insides start to turn. Waves of nausea flowed over him, his heart was racing, and he was perspiring profusely. He had never been in a fight before, not even in high school. As a kid he was well liked, and if he got into trouble, he could usually talk himself out of it. He started thinking about his chances of getting back alive.

By a tap on the shoulder and a wink, John was signaled by the man next to him that it was time to start the operation. John nodded in the affirmative. The stream provided good cover from the trees and brush along the bank. They crept up very silently from that cover to within easy distance of the village. There were a couple of guards armed with spears at the entrance to the gate. At a signal from the leader, Stevens, two of John's party approached the guards, hugging the wall and staying in the shadows. When they were within quick striking distance of the guards, they drew their bronze knives and quickly slit the poor men's throats. The attackers then quietly laid the slain guards on the ground in the shadows.

The group then crouched and quickly entered the village. They stealthily ran between the village houses. At the same time, the other group had snuck into the village from the opposite south gate. Each group was to force entry into its target house at approximately the same time, make their capture, and escape. The problem was that there was no way to tell what time it was, and therefore the timing of the operation was problematic at best. Any signal from one group to the other using sound would arouse the village. A visual signal in the dark even illuminated by the partial moon that night or the village fires, would not have been seen clearly. Therefore, the chance that one group would see the opposite target house surrounded was uncertain. And the slightest mistake by either group could spell doom to both.

Just as John's group was waiting to make entry into its target house, they heard a commotion on the other side of the holy structure. They knew they had to act; three men, including John, quickly forced their way into the darkened target house. The others stood guard around the house. They grabbed an unidentified person in the dark, and after a short struggle, they placed a bag over his body, almost completely covering him.

As they ran out of the house, two of the sentries they had posted outside the house yelled, "We have been discovered! Get out, and run!" They heard screams from the other side of the village and clanging of metal upon metal. As John turned to run for the nearest gate, a village warrior with a black beard was raising a large battle ax to bring down on his skull. John froze with fear. At that moment, one of his companions lunged at the enemy warrior, knocking him to the ground. He watched as the man pulled a knife from his belt and stabbed the warrior repeatedly in the chest. Blood gushed out of each wound with each thrust.

With Stevens, the prisoner, and three others of their party, John watched as three of their group formed a defensive line to face enemy spears as they made their escape. One of the three was quickly run through. The other two fought the spearmen savagely, with two of the enemy falling to spear and sword. The last enemy spearman was disemboweled with a sword. John's group of raiders ran as quickly as they could for the gate and the cover of the river. Stevens was on one side of their prisoner, and the youngest man in the group was on the other. John was behind them. As they sprinted for the gate, they could see that it was being closed by several of the village warriors.

Stevens screamed, "Go through them! Go through them!"

John could see Stevens and his companion, with their prize between them, yelling a loud shrill war cry as they raised their swords. When they started going through the gate, Stevens and the young man brought their swords down hard and fast on the warriors trying to close them. Screams of pain came from the enemy warriors as John ran past. They made their escape partly because of the distraction created by the other group of infiltrators.

The three of them and their hostage reached the stream and made their way west to the crest of the hill that overlooked the village. From that vantage point, they could see their brothers in the light of torches, fighting hard to retreat from the village. It seemed that more and more warriors from the village were gathering to assault that group. Bodies were being maimed and heads crushed, and John and his group could do nothing to help them. A couple of their village's group did escape and reached John's group, but without a prisoner

Master Stevens sized up the situation and announced, "We had better travel tonight. We need to put distance between them and us before dawn. If we can reach our village, we'll be safe. I want two on each side of our prisoner at all times. Walk quickly and as silently as possible." With that order, Stevens took the lead and started out, not looking back. John was in front behind Stevens. The youngster and another warrior flanked the prisoner. The remaining members of their group walked behind to form a rear guard.

Stevens said of their fallen comrades, "They died serving God, and heaven will be their reward." So they made their way west at night along the treacherous trails with their captive.

By dawn, they reached their village. As they entered their village through the main eastern gate, a cheer among the residents went up. They proudly marched their bag-cloaked captive to the central plaza. Then, with great joy, the men untied the bag and removed it. Their captive turned out to be an adolescent boy who was dressed only in his nightclothes. He was mumbling something quite incomprehensible.

The village people took him into their church. The captive seemed to be quite afraid. His eyes were open wide, sweat of fear dripped from his brow. He was hypersensitive to every noise or gesture, responding as a scared cornered dog.

Stevens asked him, "In the name of God and Jesus Christ, what are your people planning? When are they going to attack? Speak!"

When he did not answer the first time, they showed him the cross and hit him with the flat side of a sword.

The captive yelled, "We must kill all the infidels who did not accept God and the prophet." He broke free and ran out of the church. The men followed him with swords and spears. They cornered him at the base of the wall. He would not surrender and yelled, "God is great!" and ran directly onto a spear point. The young man died impaled on the spear, which was held by a shocked adolescent male from their own village.

An elder of the village said, "He was a brave boy, but he was condemned to damnation for not accepting our Lord Jesus Christ!" The village became quite nervous as they still did not know the plans of the village to the east. The people began whispering and pointing to the dead boy. "Now they will surely attack to avenge him." Stevens then spoke, "Let's give thanks to those who have returned and ask the almighty to accept into his bosom the souls our departed brethren. Hallowed be thy name." And with that the people crossed themselves and bowed in prayer. They had lost good men in the raid. All this was quite troubling to John. Attacking another village with the goal of hostage taking and loose men in the process. Yes, he thought to himself, salvation only comes from accepting Jesus, but to kill or be willing to die on one's own accord in the name of a belief other than Christian was alien to him.

CHAPTER 4

Defense

The village started making preparations for defense. They knew that the raid would only incite the enemy to attack earlier than expected, but they didn't know exactly when and in what strength. It would be better to be prepared, in any case. The fortifications on the rock walls were strengthened. Clubs, iron-headed axes, spears, and arrows with bronze or iron points were fashioned and made ready. For the first time, John saw some shorter steel swords without hilts being sharpened. There were not many of them. And they appeared to be of ancient design.

John asked, "Where did those short swords come from?"

Stevens said, "They were taken from the heathens a long time ago." The iron swords were also being made ready. The village, being close to the spring, allowed for a fortified alleyway to lead from the village fortifications to the spring. This arrangement assured drinking water during a siege. All the animals were brought into the enclosure, and the food stores were measured. Lookouts were placed atop the wall. Two catapults were hauled out of storage in an arsenal building next to the east wall. Catapults, John remembered reading somewhere, were ancient artillery devices made of wood and metal. They had a throwing arm propelled by tightly wound rope that hit a cross beam at its height and launched a projectile. An observation post was established on a hill east of the village.

For several days, all was very quiet. Preparations were carried on every day of the quiet period. But on the fourth day, the observation post could see the glint of armor and weapons in the distance. After signaling contact, the observation post was abandoned. In a couple of hours, about a dozen enemy warriors acting as skirmishers approached the village's walls across the fields. They shouted war cries and launched javelins into the enclosure. In among the skirmishers, archers and warriors with slingshots loosed their projectiles at the ramparts. They were looking for points of weakness in the defenses.

A portion of the northern wall next to the spring appeared to be the weakest point. A group of men was seen approaching that point in the wall. They had shields, spears, axes, and swords. Behind them was another group of men positioning a crude catapult, and next to them was another group with a battering ram that had a ram-shaped head of iron. The first group with individual weapons positioned themselves fifty to one hundred yards from the wall. The group manning the catapult started bombarding the wall.

John could see them loading shot of chiseled round stones onto the basket of the catapult's throwing arm. When the weapon was fired, he could see the projectiles sail through the air. Upon impact, the wall seemed to shudder, and a cheer went up from the catapult crew. At each blow of a catapult shot, pieces of wall fell both on the inside and the outside. When the wall started showing signs of failure after repeated strikes at the same point, the men with the battering ram approached the wall. The first group provided cover for the battering ram crew.

From his position in the northeastern tower, John could see that the defenders were trying gallantly to defend that portion of the wall. They hurled stones, spears, and arrows at the attackers. John suggested to Master Stevens that the villagers put some pitch in buckets, set the pitch afire, and use the catapults to hurl the buckets onto the attackers. "Also," John said, "dip the arrows in the pitch and set them alight. You can pour buckets of boiling, flaming pitch onto the ram crews as well."

Master Stevens replied, with a laugh and a grin, "That is a great idea. We'll make it too hot for them to attack the wall." Subsequently he gave orders to other men around him to make it so.

The pitch had previously been collected in a nearby valley for use in waterproofing boats, buckets, and other items. When the pitch firebombs and arrows hit the attackers, they become human torches and ran wildly about, screaming in pain, until they collapsed. This new horror induced their comrades to run for safety. Then the battering ram caught fire and burned furiously, producing great columns of black smoke. As the crewmen ran away from the burning ram, arrows felled them.

John was the hero of the moment and gained status and prestige. He asked the chieftain of the village, what else they could expect from the attackers. The village leader replied, "They are not done, and they grant no mercy." And with that statement, a cold chill went up John's spine.

After three days, the attackers assaulted the village defenses again at three points. Master Stevens said with a sneer, "Now the real battle begins." The attackers appeared to be gathering allies, as there were many more of them. This time, they had several times the number of catapults and battering rams they'd originally had, and they used these weapons to concentrate on small sections of the wall.

John could see that this was going to be an all-out attack. The women and children were gathered into the church. All the men took up positions on the wall. The assault started as before, but simultaneously at three points of attack. When one part of the wall began to fail, the defenders strengthened it by using planks to reinforce bulging cracking battlements. Extra reinforcements were also stationed at the weakened wall. But to defend that one part of the wall, the defense of another part of the wall had to be weakened. By forcing the villagers to defend various points of the wall, the attackers hoped to penetrate the wall's defenses.

The eastern gate failed first with a large, gaping hole produced by three catapults aimed at the same point on the gate. Many enemy warriors saw this opportunity and rushed into the hole. For a moment, John was astonished to see the defenders holding the breach. Then he saw the enemy's catapults concentrate fire on the northern wall to keep the defenders' heads down and prevent them from using the hot pitch weapons. At the same time, archers and slingers fired between catapult shots at the same point. This tactic allowed two rams to be brought up to attack the same point in the wall. With each blow from a ram, a loud crash could be heard, and pieces of shattered wall were shed inside and out. Cracks formed in the wall, and then that section of the northern wall collapsed with a deafening roar. The southern wall was being assaulted in the same matter and failed at about the same time as the northern one. At that moment, hordes of enemy warriors streamed into the village.

The defenders fought valiantly to defend their homes, and families. But the attackers showed no mercy as they poured through the fortifications. John had left the tower and was in the midst of the battle, fighting with all his might. Blood covered his body, arms, and face. He had never thought that he could kill another human being. But he had done so and he must, for his home and family was in peril. His other motivation was God. He was killing for God, and he would be forgiven by the Lord for killing the infidels.

He saw Master Stevens take a blow from a mace in the head from one man. Then another opponent brought his sword down on Stevens' neck, partially severing his head from his body. John saw the church being attacked and the women and children being slaughtered as they came out. He saw Laura weeping over their children's motionless bodies.

He cried, "No, no, no! Laura! Laura!" He fought like a madman to reach her. He believed that God was on his side and would not allow his family to be slaughtered. He got to within a javelin toss of the church. He looked over in the direction of Laura and saw an enemy warrior holding her by her hair. The enemy warrior raised his battle-ax. "Laura!" John cried. The enemy warrior and Laura looked up in John's direction. The cruel warrior grinned fiendishly, and as Laura looked up at John, the warrior cleaved her chest with his ax

The warrior's vicious action pushed John into a rage of vengeance, and he rushed the warrior, ignoring all others around him. Throwing his body into the warrior with the force of an enraged bull, John hacked and sliced in brutal, bloody revenge, mutilating the man and finally killing him. There was no time for John to stop the fighting and mourn his family, for the enemy troops kept attacking him. Eventually, however, he realized that the battle was futile, and he couldn't help them or others. There were too many enemy warriors. Though his heart was furious at the death of his family, he knew that he had to escape so that he could take his revenge another day.

He fought his way to the spring down in the fortified alley. When he reached the spring, he dove in and swam into the connecting pond and made his way to the other side. Crawling out and up onto the bank, he ran up the hill and hid behind some boulders. From there, he could see the destruction of the village.

The villagers who had been captured were given the option of converting to the attackers' religion and living as slaves, or else be beheaded. A number of the villagers chose conversion and slavery. He could see Father Paul bow before his captors in acceptance. But a significant number of defenders stayed loyal to their religion and chose death. The two assistant priests would not accept the new religion. The priests walked in a dignified manner to the headsman's block, which was a piece of a wrecked catapult. They were flanked by two warriors with swords drawn. The elder of the priests seemed to be praying to his God, arms uplifted. Then he crossed himself, bent down, and presented his neck to the executioner. The ax came down quickly and accurately, and the priest's head dropped onto the ground, blood spurting from the neck. Next the younger priest also prayed and made the sign of the cross, and the scene was repeated. The headsman did his work thoroughly and efficiently with a large battle ax. The beheading block was soaked with blood and was surrounded by dismembered heads and bodies. Men, women, and children fell to the headsman.

Afterward, the church was razed to the ground. The ancient symbols of the faith were desecrated by the heathen with ax and hammer. The cemetery didn't escape, either, as headstones were overturned and defaced.

This was too much for John to endure. Whose side was God on? Why couldn't John, with God's help, save his family? John felt shame and disgust at not being able to save them. He couldn't believe it: men, women, and children brutally butchered, all in the name of God. And if they were not butchered, then they were forced to convert to an alien religion and enter slavery. John's anguish was overwhelming. None of these events made sense to him.

He thought that God would surely not let this outrage go unpunished. So he left, weeping, and followed the road out of the valley, taking with him only what he had on his person.

CHAPTER 5

The Road

After four days of walking on the dry road through rough terrain, John saw that the terrain was becoming lusher with trees, grass, and shrubs. Just over a hill, he came to another village at the crest of a hill. It was a large village whose stout wall had guard towers and several gates. Two guards were on each tower and wore colorful uniforms. They were armed with round, wooden shields and iron-tipped spears.

John passed a funeral procession coming out of the north gate and making its way to a cemetery outside the wall. In the cemetery were many stone markers with a Semitic language inscribed on them, and a freshly dug grave awaiting its occupant to be.

John entered this village among the others entering and leaving. The village had homes made of stone with timber roofs. Several larger buildings stood in the center of the community on the boundaries of a plaza. On one side of the plaza was a grand, ornate church or house of worship. On the lintel above the front door was a six-pointed star or Star of David. "It is a synagogue," John thought to himself. Was this a Jewish settlement?

In the plaza was a market, with much activity of buying and selling. People of all sizes and ages walked about, dressed in anything from the most modest of tunics to the finest of robes. Children were playing in the street, laughing and shouting under their mothers' watchful supervision. The aroma of spices, breads, cheeses, and other foods was in the air.

John went to the one of the vendors, a kindly-appearing older man with wisps of grey hair on a balding scalp, and asked, "Sir, may I have some bread? I haven't eaten in days."

The vendor asked, "Do you have any money to offer in exchange?"

John replied humbly, "No, sir, I don't have any money, but I do have a weapon and some jewelry that I could trade."

The vendor looked hard at John and said, "I'll take the bronze necklace for a loaf of bread." John gave him the necklace and took the bread, which he began eagerly to eat.

Seeing his evident hunger, the vendor asked, "Where do you come from?"

Between mouthfuls of bread, John replied, "From another village to the north."

The vendor apparently had noticed John's disheveled appearance and the bloodstains on his clothes. "If I may, what happened?" he asked.

John stopped chewing, looked up, and said in a tone of embarrassment and anxiety, "My . . . my village was wiped out and . . . and my wife and children are dead."

"I'm sorry to hear about that, but please continue. Sometimes it helps to talk about it," said the man.

Sitting on the ground, John related the story of the destruction of the village and the slaughter that followed.

The man asked, "Are you Christian?"

John nodded and added, "I am new to this land and only recently came to that village. I am not familiar with the history of this land and why such things happen."

The old merchant said, "You are now in a Hebrew settlement. We have been here since the time this land was granted to us by God." The merchant smiled. "Excuse me, young man. You're Christian and know the history of my people almost as well as I do. We have generally been tolerant of Christians, despite their persecution of us. You know that whole business with the Sanhedrin and the crucifixion of your Lord Jesus. Since that time, there have been many conquerors of my people. The empire was the most ruthless and most efficient in its rule and oppression. They almost completely destroyed our people. But we survived, anyway."

The merchant picked up a large loaf of bread and began slicing it into thick pieces and offered him a slice. "Others came and went—Christian, other pagan religions, and the new religion. The new religion is different, but it has many of the same ideas as Christianity and Judaism. However, its followers claim that a special knowledge was revealed to them by their prophet. Strange . . . they are so similar and yet so different. Anyway, no one nation has been able to replace the empire. The result has been various city states with changing allegiances that war constantly with each other."

The old man smiled at John, who had finished the bread. "Our rabbi has brought up an old argument recently. He says that the Christians worship of a man who called himself the son of God is blasphemous and should not be tolerated. We all know he means Jesus. So be careful, my boy. A lot of us heard the rabbi, but have decided to let it be. However, there are those much younger who have been bitten by the zeal of a fanatic. So be careful what you say to strangers here."

To this bit of news, John replied, "Thank you, sir, for your concern and the information. What you tell me is familiar . . . yet this place isn't. I feel like I have been here before, but perhaps not under these circumstances. What is down the road?" John pointed in the direction opposite the one he had traveled.

To this question, the old man smiled and continued slicing more loaves. "Down the road you will find more villages— some like this one and some Christian. Others will be pagan, and others possibly of the new religion. So choose your friends carefully and wisely. Death doesn't need much of an excuse to claim you in this land. Eventually you will come to a city. It is Christian now. There you will find shelter, food, and maybe a living. Good luck to you, young man, and may God keep you."

John thanked the man profusely and left the town. "The old man would have made a fine Christian," he thought. "I will pray for him even though he is a Jew."

He walked for several more days and came to another village, which was fortified with a large wood and rock stockade. He entered among a crowd through the main gate with guards armed with shields and spears on either side. The wooden houses were built around a central stone meeting house, or perhaps a temple, John thought. The temple had classical Corinthian columns in front and rough-hewn stone side walls that reminded him of a cave.

On the lintel on the meeting house was an engraving of a human figure that was slaying a bull, and a snake, a dog, a raven, and a scorpion were arrayed around the central figure. This image struck John as unusual, but he recalled having seen a similar icon pictured in seminary. Then it came to him: this must be a place of worship of the god Mithras.

John recalled that the god was worshipped by an ancient Roman cult similar to Christianity that arose at about the same time as Christianity. It was adopted by the Romans from an early Persian religion. In fact, Christianity adopted many of Mithraism's holy dates and symbology. The date of Christmas, December 25, is actually the date that the birth of Mithras was celebrated. The date was adopted by Christianity as the date to remember the birth of Jesus. Later it became the birth date of Jesus in traditional Christianity.

He remembered that several lines of modern evidence have shown that Christ was more than likely born in the spring, probably around the middle of April. John thought that the Mithras cult had died out at the time Christianity became the state religion of Rome. Originally the meeting places of this cult were caves. Seeing the temple now, he guessed that the worship sites must have evolved to a more traditional type of temple that had hints of a cave in the architecture.

John circled the temple, admiring the artwork and symbols. Under the eves of the roof of the temple John studied several icons. One shows Mithras supporting on his shoulder the great sphere of the cosmos, much like Atlas holding the world. Another scene showed Mithras supporting the starry sky contained beneath his flying cape, and another showed him emerging from the top of a round-shaped rock or egg with a snake entwined around it.

John decided to explore the village more completely. The community was laid out on a grid pattern. One area of the village appeared to be a business section or forum with shops of various kinds. Items including clothing, food, weapons, and religious artifacts could be bought and sold. Each vendor seemed to specialize in one particular kind of merchandise. He noted a blacksmith shop that seemed busy. Another area of the village was residential. Women were talking with one another, and children were playing in the streets. In another area was a barracks and an arsenal. Soldiers in uniforms of brightly colored cloth and leather breastplates, with chain mail shirts and bronze greaves, stood guard and participated in drills. They were using large, Roman-type, three-quarter-length shields called scutums and steel swords of a length that he had seen before of shorter length.

John could see various catapults stationed around the yard. The stockade had guard towers in every corner and one tower placed midway along the wall. Each guard tower was manned by two soldiers armed with pilum, the Roman javelin with a wooden staff and an iron shank and point. John had read that the iron shank was pliable and would bend if it hit the ground or an enemy shield, thus making it impossible to hurl back at the thrower. Another area of the village had a large building that was used as a granary. The central plaza contained a well that John guessed everyone in the village used.

All the people John could see were wearing brightly colored tunics and togas. They were friendly but suspicious of strangers. Their language was a little different and more formal. All the men were armed with steel daggers or Roman double-bladed swords called gladius Hispiniensis. The women wore makeup and jewelry made of gold and precious stones.

Walking to the forum, John bartered for food and a flask of wine and paid for them with the few items he had left. He did not talk much and instead indicated what he wanted through sign. As he was leaving the village, he noticed a cemetery outside the wall on the south side of the village. It had many markers and a few fairly large mausoleums. On the edge of the cemetery, there appeared to be an altar with burn marks. John didn't know whether this item was meant for sacrifices to Mithras in honor of the dead or was a cremation site for the dead.

After several days on the desert road, he came across a man lying on the side of the road. He had been attacked and was badly injured, with bruises, cuts, and slashes on his arms, legs, abdomen, chest, and face. Some of the blood from the wounds had dried, making John think that the injuries had occurred a few hours to a day ago. Some of the man's possessions were scattered around the nearby road and hillside. John went to him, asking, "Are you all right? What happened?"

The man, who was middle-aged and stout in build, replied in a dry, trembling voice. "Sir, I was attacked and robbed. I am in pain and cannot walk. Can you help me?"

"Yes, I will," said John, kindly smiling. "That is what a Christian is supposed to do." He gave the man most of his water and some bread from his meager supplies. Then John examined the man as best he could, cleaned his wounds, and dressed them with some linen he found scattered around.

The man appeared upset as he began relating his story. "I was going home when several men approached me. It was . . . yesterday . . . no . . . the day before. My sense of time is off."

"That is OK," John said. : You are all right now. Your attackers are not anywhere around."

"When they were within an arm's length," the man continued, "they drew their swords and threatened to kill me if I didn't give them money and anything else I had of value. I told them I was just a cloth and leather merchant and had nothing of value. They ripped the packs off my donkeys and searched them, and they vandalized everything I had, looking for what I didn't have. When they realized that there was nothing worth stealing, they started beating me. After a while, I passed out. When I awoke, I had blood in my eyes. My jaw was swollen and sore. My tongue found a couple of teeth missing. I couldn't get up because my hips and legs were in extreme pain. I fear they broke my legs."

John helped the man to his feet and encouraged him to walk a few steps. "Your legs don't seem to be broken," he said gently. "But you do have severe bruises and cuts on them."

"Oh, thank God," the man said. "Blessed be the savior Jesus Christ for that miracle."

From the amount of goods scattered nearby, John concluded that the bandits hadn't made off with everything, so the man would be able to use those items to barter for more supplies from passersby. John worked quickly to set up a camp with a fire and shelters fashioned from stones, palm branches, and textiles he found around the site.

For several days, John stayed with the merchant, dressing his wounds daily and offering companionship. As John would change the man's bandages, he told the man about his life.

"I come from a village to the north," John said. "It was destroyed by another village, and my wife and children were slaughtered." Tears poured down John's face as he related his story to the injured man. "I could do nothing. I have been a deeply religious man all of my life and have always put my trust in the Lord Jesus. So why did God allow this to happen? Why?"

With a little grunt of pain, the merchant responded, "Please, not so tight a bandage. That's better. I'll tell you, my friend, we never know what is in store for us or our loved ones and why. My people have been persecuted by our brethren for centuries. We believe in the same Lord Jesus. But, nonetheless, we are hunted down and killed or forced to convert to their form of Christianity."

John interrupted. "Their form? You are Christian?"

"Yes."

"Then why are you persecuted by other Christians?"

"Because . . . Are you the kind of Christian who abhors the ways of other Christians and will kill them if they are different or at the very least make it his duty to convert them to his way?"

"No, no," John said, hoping he sounded reassuring. "We are all brothers and sisters in the body of Christ, and one should not kill or harm a fellow Christian."

The merchant asked sternly, "Will you keep my secret until death?"

"Yes, by all that is holy and sacred in Christ himself, I swear that I will never betray you."

"Good. Then I will tell you. I hope what I say will give you a little understanding and solace. Also, I detect in you a merciful and kind man, for otherwise you would not have stopped to help me." The man lay back on a cushion and closed his eyes as he continued.

"The Christian group I belong to does not have its books included in the Holy Bible. We are considered to be heretics. You may know us as Gnostics. We did at one time comprise a large portion of Christianity. However, our writings were banned. We were hunted down, killed, or forced to convert to the orthodox view of Christ. There are very few of us left, but we still exist."

The man opened his eyes to look directly into John's face. "We believe Jesus to be the ultimate teacher of knowledge and wisdom. He has imparted to us a special mystical knowledge or enlightenment. We hope that some day the other Christians will come to realize that gift from God. We believe that knowledge is more important than faith itself, and we believe that salvation is due to knowledge of oneself. Therefore, my boy, learn as much as you can. Learn from the sacred texts and others; learn about our world and ourselves." As the man stared at John, he saw that the younger man's face showed excitement. In an almost shy tone, the merchant asked, "Would . . . would you like to read some of my gospels?"

John was astounded. He had read about the Gnostics in seminary, but to meet one and talk with one was quite different. He was curious about the other gospels, and the merchant didn't seem like a heretic.

Wide-eyed, his mouth falling open, John was mute for a moment. Then he said, "Oh, yes . . . yes, I would."

Hearing that, the merchant pulled out a leather case that was hidden beneath some other items. Opening the case, he took out a worn, leather-bound book and began reading some verses to John. John learned that the book had six gospels and other books of faith, though none of them had ever been considered canonical or included in the Christian Bible. John knew from seminary that only fragments of the Gnostics gospels and books survived. But here were the whole texts intact!

The man told John that he traveled freely between Christian and Hebrew towns to do business. The man was learned and well spoken. His business was a family enterprise, and he knew that his wife and sons would be concerned about him. When he was well enough to continue his journey, John bid him farewell and received from the man a leather bag containing several coins.

The merchant said, "This is for your kindness, compassion, and help. May God bless you."

CHAPTER 6

The City

John walked up several increasingly arid hills toward the southeast. After six days, he came to a fairly large, walled city that was flanked on two sides by deep valleys. The larger, deeper valley on the northeast side had many freestanding tombs cut from the rock or built into the walls of the valley. The city, which covered most of the hill it was built on, was surrounded by walls with battlements and fortified gates.

To John, the city seemed strangely familiar. He entered the northwestern gate and immediately found himself in a crowd in what appeared to be a bazaar. He smelled strange, exotic aromas. People dressed in a variety of clothes from the most humble to the most elegant were rushing about, talking and trading. Goods of all sorts filled the small shops in the bazaar. With some of the coins he bought a knife, a bit of rope and a change of cloths.

A large platform on the northeast edge of the city was built upon gigantic stones with large ruins upon it. Among the ruins there appeared to be small, poorly built huts. John continued to walk the alleyways and streets of the city. Some of the smells were distinctly unpleasant, partly because the residents emptied their refuse into the streets.

Small business sections were scattered among the residential sections. Along the walls John could see places where barracks had been established for the garrison of the city. He could see soldiers drilling with gladiuses, pilums, and scutums on the parade grounds of the barracks. Next to the barracks area was a blacksmith shop, which John supposed was used to repair weapons or fashion new ones, as well as to make shoes for horses.

He came to what appeared to be an inn where he hoped to stay the night. He entered a doorway and was immediately greeted by the innkeeper, an old man who was good-natured and helpful. He was grey headed and had numerous wrinkles on his face, and he wore a modest beige tunic.

John was grateful for the friendly greeting, "I do need a room, sir. What do you have to let?"

"I have a fine room at the top of stairs," the innkeeper said. "Would you like to see it?" John nodded and followed after the old man to the top of the stairs, where he unlocked a door and stepped into a room. John entered after him and saw that the room had a window overlooking the street. In one corner was a cabinet, and in another corner was a bed with clean blankets and a pillow. A small oil lamp sat on a table next to the bed. The room was modest but amply filled John's needs.

Turning to the man, John asked, "What is your price?"

The man said, "Four city coins."

"How about two city coins?"

"No," said the inn keeper. "But what about three?"

"Agreed," John said. "Now where can I wash up?"

"The washroom and the honey closet are down the hall and to the left. A honey pot is under the bed, and you are required to empty it yourself every morning. May I ask how long you are staying?"

"I don't know at this time. May I keep the room as long as I need it?"

"Yes, by all means, as long as you keep paying for the services of the room." "

"I would like to stay until I can find some way of supporting myself and getting some answers," John said. "Do you offer meals here as well?"

"No, no, I am sorry to say we do not provide food here, but there is a fine café I can recommend," said the old innkeeper. He gave John directions to a café a few blocks from the inn.

John made his way to the café without much difficulty. The streets were busy with people rushing about and children playing. The café could be recognized by the sign hanging above the entryway, a boars head and tankard. He entered and immediately heard a din of laughter, conversations, and music. A maid greeted him and led him to a table in the corner. He ordered a good meal—bread, a tuber of some sort, and meat that reminded him of Greek gyros. With the meal came a glass of red wine.

His stomach full, John started feeling warmer and more satisfied. He watched the other patrons and thought that the place was not really different from his home. In his mind he suddenly saw the faces of his wife and children, and he grimaced angrily. Although he had shed many tears in mourning for them, now he thought only of finding a way to avenge his family's deaths. He believed that God and Christ would not allow such a crime to go unpunished.

To keep himself from dwelling on the lost lives of his family—lives he could never repair—John began reviewing in his mind all the things he had seen and heard since arriving in this strange land. He had seen no technology beyond swords, spears, archery equipment, and ancient siege machines. Everyone seemed to get around by foot or horse. There were no cars, airplanes, trains, telephones, radios, guns, or any other of the many inventions to which he had become accustomed. Everyone seemed to live in fairly independent communities and had strong faiths in their God or gods.

"I must find some way to win for Christ the others in this land," John thought, "and I must avenge my family. Their deaths cannot go unpunished."

Angrily thrusting a coin onto the table to pay for his meal, John made his way back to the inn and fell asleep.

John awoke early to the sound of a rooster crowing. He gathered the things he needed for that day and started out to explore the city. According to the agreement he had made with the proprietor so that he could stay as long as he wished, John was required to deposit a third of the rent in a box with his name at the front desk before he left on any excursions for the day. The rest he would deposit at night with the innkeeper.

The streets were already filled with pedestrians, merchants, and a variety of other people. After some time, he came to a large, two-story building with a caduceus, the staff of Aesculapius, on the lintel. From this ancient symbol of medicine or healing, John deduced that this building was a hospital. He was curious because he remembered that his friend Mark was a doctor.

As he went through the doorway, an awful stench of rotting flesh, urine, and feces accosted him. He saw no medical personnel in clean white uniforms or lab coats. And there didn't appear to be nurses of the type he was familiar with. He did see a few women, but most of the aides seemed to be young men. He also saw a few older, bearded men who wore much finer tunics, robes, and togas. The older gentlemen, he surmised, were the doctors.

John walked through the hallways and noticed that the building was divided into wards. All the windows were shuttered and closed. One ward appeared to contain people with various injuries from weapons or falls. Fractures were splinted with pieces of wood on either side of the limb. Compound fractures or open breaks were treated the same way, but many seemed to have become infected. John guessed that these patients either died or had their infected limbs amputated.

Another ward was filled with people who had awful, pus-oozing sores, which he observed were dressed with compresses and plasters that smelled as bad as the wounds themselves. Yet another ward appeared to be an obstetrical ward, which appeared to be staffed primarily by midwives. John had read that in this period of time, half to three quarters of the women died from what was called childbed fever. John recalled that the women had a slightly better chance of living if the midwives washed their hands at least occasionally.

A fourth ward was reserved for people with coughs. Some appeared to be in acute distress, breathing hard and rapidly, while attendants wiped their sweating brows with damp cloths. Others were coughing up blood and pieces of tissue. John was surprised that no attempt was made to isolate these patients. Another ward was for the patients with nausea, vomiting, and diarrhea. Attempts were made to keep fluids down these patients, but usually to no avail. Some vomited blood or had stools that were mostly blood. These patients died a terrible death rather quickly. Attendants had to run to keep up with the over flowing honey pots. A large number of these patients simply succumbed to dehydration, as the only way they had to try and hydrate them was with water (usually polluted) by mouth, and other potions. The saddest patients were the children, who died in their weeping mothers arms from dehydration. The honey pots and soiled dressings were taken to the back of the building and dumped in an empty lot. John noticed that the doctors were treating patients with the ancient method of bloodletting using leeches. The aides were also administering various noxious-smelling potions that John guessed had been prescribed by the physicians.

There really wasn't an operating room. The doctors would not have gone in there anyway as they considered surgery beneath them. Instead, they would consult barber-surgeons who would do various operations without anesthesia in the wards behind temporary screens. The patient was held down by five brawny attendants. The patient was given wine mixed with some herbal juices that acted as a type of sedation. A leather-wrapped dowel was placed between the patient's teeth at the beginning of the procedure. The surgical instruments were crude and simple. Scalpels had to be sharpened before each operation. A saw was used to divide bones in amputations. Various probes were used to gauge the depth of wounds and to search for foreign objects in tissue. Assortments of knives were used to cut muscle, tendon, and sinew. Trephines were in the surgeon's tool kit on the skull or brain. It was thought that if the surgeon opened an area in the skull to let bad demons out, the patient would stop having seizures and would no longer be possessed. Wounds were repaired with suture made from hair obtained from horse's tails or long, thin, braided wool and, occasionally, silk threaded on long bronze needles. Nearly all of the wounds after surgery became infected and produced what the barber-surgeons called "laudable pus."

John noticed that there were a number of holy men walking among the patients. Wearing simple robes of coarse, woven cloth, they carried Bibles and had bronze crosses on chains around their necks. At patients' bedsides, the holy men appeared to be performing religious rites. It seemed to John that prayer and exorcism were an integral part of giving health care. He talked to some of the health workers and was shocked to discover that a high percentage of the patients died. He surmised primarily from infection. They thought disease was spread by vapors. Hence, they tried to keep the vapors out by shutting the windows. The belief was that all of illness was due to the vapors or demons. Therefore, holy men were used trying to exorcise the demons from the sick.

When John tried to suggest to a doctor and a couple of others that they could decrease the death rate by washing their hands and boiling water, they laughed at him. When he told them that disease was actually caused by microscopic germs, they started calling him a witch. At that point, he decided that the better part of valor was a retreat at this time. He realized that it would be nearly impossible to convince them that their beliefs were false.

He continued his tour of the city. Not far from the hospital was a pool. He noticed a lot of people bathing in the pool and that many had afflictions of different types, withered extremities, paralysis, and others. Farther on, he came to a large, domed church next to a rock quarry. A large door made of oak bore a large cross. John decided not to enter at this time and come back to it later. Past the church, he saw another building that had apparently been a temple to another god, and next to that building was what appeared to have been a synagogue. The six-pointed Star of David was defaced on the lintel, but it was still discernable. John looked inside this building's open door and saw that the building was evidently being used as a storehouse with amphora stacked to the ceiling. Farther along was what appeared to be another synagogue that was being used as a granary!

Some distance away from the second synagogue was a large building in front of which many young men dressed in fine tunics were coming and going. Most of the men had books and scrolls in their arms. Small groups were standing around a courtyard, engaged in heavy discussion. John decided to go inside. He entered one area that turned out to be an amphitheater. On the stage of the amphitheater was a professor who was giving a lecture to a full crowd. Interestingly, on the side of the stage was a holy man who was also listening intently. John decided to take a seat and listen to the lecture. The professor was describing the perfect crystal spheres of the universe and how the planets, the moon, and the sun revolved around the earth. This was odd, John thought, because the professor was describing the ancient view of the universe according to Aristotle or Ptolemy. Was this a class in astronomy or mythology? No mention was made of Copernicus, Galileo, or Newton and their contributions, and John wondered why not. As he listened, he discovered that these people actually viewed the universe in this way. He got up and went down the hall to another classroom where the teacher was discussing biology. John stayed for a while to observe the class. He noticed that there was the ever-present holy man on the side, watching and listening.

The professor said," God created every plant, animal, and man over 6000 years ago. Every animal and plant lives according to God's will. Man benefits from relationships with animals and plants. Monkeys and apes are beasts that appear similar to man, but behave like beasts and live in the wilderness. They are beasts, whereas man was created in God's image."

At that point, a student asked a question. "If monkeys and apes appear similar to man, and if God created man in his image, then are monkeys and apes also similar to God?"

Before the professor could answer the question, someone yelled out "Blasphemy!" and the student who had asked the question was immediately taken into custody by two soldiers that were stationed at entrance to the classroom. John was shocked at the radical action taken against the student. He agreed that comparing God to animals or even attempting to suggest that animals are similar to man and God is blasphemy.

It was getting close to lunchtime. Other students were getting out lunches that they carried in cloth sacks. John made his way to a side street and found lunch at a sidewalk café. Fascinated by what he had seen and observed that morning, he considered what it meant. He finished his meager lunch and returned to the school to see if he could learn more about where he was.

He entered a different classroom and sat down. In this class, the subject was architecture. He noticed the ever-present holy man next to the teacher. No controversial subjects came up during this period. He made his way to another class and sat down. Again, the holy man was present. This class was about warfare and history. From this class, John was able to learn that after the breakup of the Roman Empire, the church gained dominance in society. A few hundred years after the fall of the empire, a new religion from the East conquered this city. All of Christendom, at the behest of the Pope in Rome, mounted a crusade to take back the holy land. After many years of bloody struggle, only parts of the holy land had returned to the one true religion.

There had been centuries of constant warfare between the new religion, Christianity, Judaism, and a few surviving pagan religions. Very little, if any, interaction occurred between any of the religions or cultures. John learned that the city was conquered and re-conquered many times by each religious group. It seemed that as one side took an area the holy sites were converted to the conquerors' religion by tearing down and rebuilding the buildings, or the sites were used for a new function. People spent much time and effort in trying to convert or fight the heathen and the enemies of the faith.

John wandered down another hall, entered a classroom, and found himself in a philosophy class. Again, the holy man was at the front of the class. This class concentrated on the philosophers of ancient Greece, Rome, and the church. The origins of the universe and man's place in it were considered only in relationship to God— which, as the students were told, is only right because man would not exist without God.

John moved on to a separate building and found it to be the medical school of the university. There were no dissections, as it was the policy of the church not to desecrate the dead. All of the anatomy was based on ancient Greek and Roman texts. Hippocrates' writings and those of Claudius Galen, the great Roman physician, were the sources of knowledge for diagnosis and treatment. However, not all the ancient knowledge of these two fathers of medicine was utilized if it in some way went counter to the church. To his amazement, astrology was also taught in the school. Prescriptions and treatments for disease were a mix of astrological mysticism, bloodletting (to get the bad humors out), and the administration of various potions made of herbs and other substances. Every class had a holy man standing up front next to the professor.

It was evening when John walked back to his room. He was tired, hungry, and quite perplexed by what he had observed that day. He had studied some science in school and thought that even with his basic understanding; he was far more advanced than these people. If he had to live here in this place and this time, maybe he can make use of his advanced understanding of science.

Chapter 7

A Calling, a Business

John started thinking that if he could reinvent the cannon and other relative modern weapons; those would seem to be super weapons to people living in this world. He could be the savior and defender of Christianity. With weapons like these, he could spread the faith. He could also avenge his family's murder. Once that was done, he could reinvent other devices for the benefit of this society and the faith.

The first thing had to do was to make gunpowder, as it would provide the energy needed for the weapons he envisioned. He had to draw on memories of basic high school chemistry, and he would have to experiment. He knew gunpowder had three primary components: sulfur, charcoal, and saltpeter. The charcoal would be easy to get from the people's fireplaces. A traveler he met at the café for lunch was from a small village to the east and told him that there was a geologically active area in the vicinity of a large salt sea. He surmised that he could get the sulfur from that location. The saltpeter could be extracted from guano. The best place to look for guano is in caves. He would also need a workshop and helpers. With a plan in mind, John went to sleep.

The next morning, John awoke refreshed and eager. He quickly cleaned up and got dressed. Half running, he went down to the lobby.

He asked the innkeeper, "Who do I need to talk to about starting a business and getting support for it?"

The innkeeper replied, "Is it a good idea? I will contribute, but you also will have to get permission from the city authorities."

"And who is that?"

The innkeeper answered reverently and somewhat hesitantly, "Archbishop Gregory. His Holiness lives in the palace next to the old Roman citadel."

John wandered down the city's streets, getting lost several times before he asked for some help. He found the palace on the far side of a large, cobblestone plaza. The building was magnificent. He slowly made his way to the palace, captured by its magnificence and power. The whole building was built of ocher marble, glistening in the bright day. It had Ionic columns around a large portico. It sat on top of three stacked platforms in a stepped pyramid style, with a flight of steps to each level, totaling twenty steps. Wings jutted from the sides of the central portion of the building, whose main doors were of bronze, each with religious relief's set in their panels.

John stood awestruck for several minutes until the magic of the sight passed. He ascended the stairs, and as he was about to enter the doorway, he was immediately stopped by two soldiers with gladiuses in scabbards at their sides. They each held a scutum and a pilum and wore a curious mix of ancient Roman armor and medieval plate armor. The armor looked like it had been repaired many times, but it still retained the appearance of power and authority. The soldiers also wore Templar crosses on their breastplates.

The older of the two soldiers commanded, "Halt! Citizen, please state your business here."

John straightened up and tried to look as important as possible before he said, "I request an audience with Archbishop Gregory on a very important matter."

The younger the two soldiers asked, "Do you have an appointment?"

John shook his head in the negative. The soldiers promptly took him by both arms and escorted him off the palace grounds. One of them said, "You will need a letter of introduction from someone of importance who can also arrange an appointment with the archbishop."

Saddened and confused, John made his way back to the inn.

When he got back to the inn, he found the innkeeper at work with the books at the front desk. John walked up to him, tapped the desk, and asked, "Do you know some important person who could write a letter of introduction for me and arrange an appointment with the archbishop?"

The old man replied, "Why, yes, I do. That would be the commissioner of merchants."

The next day, John was introduced to the commissioner as he was making his rounds, collecting licensing fees from the merchants and innkeepers. The commissioner invited John to his house that night to discuss the matter.

John knocked on the door and was greeted by a servant. He was led into a medium-sized waiting room. The commissioner entered and greeted John with a hearty handshake. "Welcome, my man," he said. He was a clean-shaven, portly man, wearing a scarlet tunic and toga befitting his rank. His hair was black with a hint of grey beginning along the edges and sprinkled throughout the rest.

John said, "Sir, I appreciate very much your willingness to see and hear me." He explained how he could help spread the faith and defend it with some inventions. He was very careful to note that these devices would in no way offend God. He outlined his need for a workshop, supplies, craftsmen, money, and a place to live. He concluded, "Sir, in return for support, I promise a percentage of the commissions that I would receive for developing and building such devices as return on investment in them. And, if you know of any business people who would be interested in investing in this venture, I would be grateful for introductions."

The commissioner said, "Master John, I do know of some men of means that would heartily support you and invest in these ventures. And I am one of them. You have vision, insight, and an extremely persuasive manner."

John, both gracious and practical about the situation, replied, "Sir, that is excellent. But I have another problem. From what I understand, I need permission from the archbishop. How can I get an audience to see him and present the idea?"

The commissioner smiled and said, "My boy, leave that to me. I know the archbishop well, and I can arrange all that, along with a letter of introduction. Now may I have the have the honor of your staying for dinner with me and my family?"

"Sir, if I am not an intrusion into your family affairs tonight, I would be honored," replied John, though he was certainly surprised at the invitation.

They walked down a long hallway to the large dining hall. John saw a large, long oak dining table with chairs. The room was decorated with paintings and statues, all clothed. The commissioner's wife, a dignified, handsome woman in a fine yellow dress, was seated at one end of the table. Two of his sons, clothed in their finest tunics, were seated on one side of the table, and John was seated next to the commissioner's beautiful daughter, Catherine. John noticed immediately that she had olive-toned, fine features under auburn hair. Her pale blue dress was of the finest cloth, and she radiated warmth and grace.

The commissioner took his place at the head of the table. The meal consisted of roasted lamb, bread, fruit and wine which was served, as John assumed, by a butler and maids. During the dinner, the commissioner took great pride in talking about John's plans, and his involvement in it. However, John saw or heard very little of the dinner as he was totally taken by the beautiful woman next to him. He barely spoke and was both infatuated and embarrassed by the commissioner's daughter. He noticed that she seemed genuinely intrigued by him as well, by a smile, a glance.

John left the commissioner's house with an odd feeling that he hadn't felt in a long time. He went back to the inn and tried to sleep but could not.

He tossed and turned, thinking about Catherine and feeling ill at ease because of the memory of his wife and children. He prayed and prayed to God for guidance. What was he to do? Should he wallow in grief for the rest of his life, or was God giving him a new chance at life and love? Subtly, gently, Laura's voice seemed to speak to him: "It's all right, it's all right . . . it's all right." Yes, he could love again and be happy and yet honor and love Laura and his children. It was all right, and Laura was telling him it was. With this thought, John was at last able to rest.

On the following morning, John went to the commissioner's house, as instructed. The commissioner gave him a formal letter of introduction to the archbishop, as well as some pointers on etiquette in the archbishop's presence. The commissioner had arranged for an appointment with the archbishop on the following day. Things were moving quickly. John did, however, ask the commissioner how his daughter was. The commissioner seemed a little bemused by the question, but he answered in the affirmative as to his daughter's state of health.

The next morning came, bright with expectations. John had bought some new clothes, the day before. He was careful in his preparations for his audience with the archbishop. He made up drawings and specifications of some of the devices he intended to build so that he could show them to the archbishop. Carefully he put those drawings in a leather case along with some notes. When he was sure that he looked his best and that he had all that he needed to take with him, he left the inn.

He was excited and nervous at the same time. He could see himself becoming a very important person in this city and world. He made his way to the palace, walked up the steps, and presented the letter of introduction to the guards.

The older one said, "We have been expecting you sir, so please follow me."

He led John down a long, marble hallway to a huge room, where the archbishop was seated on a large gilded throne at the farthest end. Many attendants and courtiers were in the room, which was decorated with paintings and sculptures. Most of the artwork was religious representations of saints, Biblical scenes, and the like. A large, gold-leaf cross was suspended from the ceiling above the throne.

The archbishop wore a purple tunic and robes. His clothes appeared to be of the finest cloth and silk detailed with golden designs along the edges. He was clean shaven and had grey hair showing around the edges of his miter. John had the distinct impression that the archbishop resembled Caesar.

John strode to the front of the throne and made a long, deep bow, presenting his letter of introduction.

After glancing at the letter, Archbishop Gregory said, "Arise, my son, and state your business."

"May it please your Grace that I, as a faithful follower of Christ, have thought long and hard about how to defend and spread the faith. It is with such goals in mind that I've been blessed with an idea, a plan, and a way of accomplishing those goals."

John outlined his plans and showed drawings of the devices to the archbishop and several others in attendance. All of them asked questions, to which John had well-prepared answers. Archbishop Gregory very much approved of John and his ideas and gave him his full support. He said that the state would provide John with a workshop, skilled workers, a house, and an endowment. John left the palace feeling giddy and important.

CHAPTER 8

Expedition

The workshop provided to John had areas for metalworking, alchemy, carpentry, and stone working. He was also given a modest residence in an influential area of the city and, most importantly, a sizable endowment on which to live, buy supplies and equipment, and to pay workers assigned to him. John's first task was to organize the shop and to assign duties. His next chore was to organize an expedition to gather some of the needed raw materials.

But first, he wanted to see the commissioner's daughter. As etiquette required, John had to ask the commissioner for permission to see and court his daughter. After he was greeted at the commissioner's front door and shown into the seating room, he hesitantly said to the commissioner, "Sir, I hope that I do not offend you with my lack of station, but I admire your daughter Catherine quite a lot. If it pleases you, and if she approves it herself as well, may I have permission to court her? "

After a pause, the commissioner said, "John, it is true you have no station now, but you are an energetic, imaginative, and aggressive lad. I believe that you will make a name for yourself and go far. Yes, you may court my daughter—that is, if she approves."

A servant escorted John to the garden, where Catherine was tending flowers. She was wearing a golden-yellow dress and had flowers in her hair. Her eyes met John's when he entered the garden. He said, "Hello, my lady. I have asked your father for permission to see you. He has granted it. I would be honored if you would accept my attentions and would allow me to court you."

Catherine appeared surprised, though she also remained composed. "Master John, in our world, courtship is often the prelude to marriage. And if this is what you eventually intend, I expect certain things from a man. Are you prepared to provide them?"

Taken a little back by this response, he looked at her sincerely and said, "Catherine, ever since I saw you at that dinner the other night, I haven't been able to get you out of my mind. If you expect love, respect, and honor, that I can guarantee. Anything else I cannot."

"John that is exactly what I expect. Yes, of course you can court me, but I also expect you to win my hand properly and prove yourself," She smiled at him and touched his hand very gently as she said, "But we must also follow tradition and respect our parents' wishes. I would like to meet your parents sometime."

"My father passed away a long time ago," John said regretfully, "and . . . I do not know where my mother is . . . now."

Catherine said, "I am sorry. Was your father killed in battle . . . and your mother taken as a slave?"

"No, no, my father wasn't—he died of natural causes. My mother is still living, but I really don't know where she is now. Yet I feel certain that she would approve of you."

"I am sorry about the loss of your father," Catherine said. "He must have been a good and noble man. He will be waiting for you in heaven. I hope to meet your mother someday."

"So do I . . . if possible. I wish we could spend more time together right now, but I have to leave on an expedition to look for some materials to start to build my . . . our new life. Forgive me for having to leave so soon." He kissed her hand good-bye.

She maintained her veneer of restraint. Then she said, "I understand, so safely return, John."

He turned and left the garden.

The archbishop gave John a squadron of armored warriors as protection, as well as a string of twelve horses. A group of about twenty-five workmen also accompanied the expedition. Besides the soldiers' weapons, John and his workmen carried their own weapons, as well as shovels, picks, and various other tools. The expedition carried tents, supplies, and enough rations to last over two weeks.

John planned to go into the wilderness east of the city and then southeast toward the salt sea. The expedition started early the next morning, following a long road that led from their city to a more ancient city in the valley of the salt sea. They occasionally passed other travelers, some on horseback and some afoot. The road went up hills and around hills, but generally had an east-southeast, downhill direction. Occasionally, they passed caves. John usually sent a scout into the cave to see if there was any guano. Most of the time, the scout would return empty-handed.

One evening, John spied a cloud circling a distant hill, and he thought it might be bats. The next day, he sent some scouts to that area, and they returned with sacks of guano. The expedition headed toward that cave the following day. When they reached the cave, the workmen made preparations to mine the guano. They spent two days bagging guano and tied the bags onto the horses. After the mining was completed, they continued on their way toward the salt sea.

One night they stopped by a pleasant little stream and made camp. John and some of the others saw a glow not far away. John also thought he heard voices and music.

He walked with several workmen and a small number of the soldiers to reconnoiter the other village or campsite that they suspected was in the area. As they crawled up over the crest of a hill, they saw five colorful tents below them. A central campfire and a group of guards were positioned around the campsite. The guards wore bronze breastplates and were armed with medium-length, curved swords and spears. In three of the tents, there appeared to be wealthy travelers. In the other two tents were more soldiers.

One of the soldiers with John said, "They are of the new religion. We should organize an attack and kill the infidels."

But John refused, saying, "That is not our purpose on this expedition. They are not bothering us, and we will not bother them." John did leave a scout to monitor the camp, with orders to warn him if it looked as though the campers were preparing to take hostile action.

When morning came, John's group packed up camp and started on their way, being careful not to draw attention to them. They avoided the city in the northwest area of the salt sea valley, staying close to the encircling hills.

One valley connected to the valley of the salt sea was like an oasis. It had trees, a stream flowing through it, caves, and wildlife. John and his men set up camp at this site. John sent scouts throughout the area after describing what he was looking for. He called it sulfur, and they called it brimstone.

After several days, one of the scouts came back, saying he found what John was looking for in the southern part of the valley. He said it was close to the site were two cities of evil had been destroyed by God in ancient times. The men of John's expedition packed all their goods and set off again. It took them several days to get to the southern end of the valley. On the way, John noticed a high plateau with what looked like ruins of fortifications on top. Around that plateau were what appeared to be ruins of a long rock wall and square fortifications spaced at intervals. In the southern end of the valley, they found fumaroles with deposits of sulfur, as well as seams of sulfur deposits in the walls of the nearby cliff. Over a period of days, they mined what they could and loaded the sulfur into bags for transport back to the city.

One of the scouts reported back late. He had found a spring lying about one hundred yards from a ruined fortification, north of a wadi called Ein Bokek on the western side of the salt sea. This fortification had probably been a saltpeter factory. Saltpeter could be used for several purposes, such as preserving food and making magic. The scout reported that saltpeter could be scraped from the floors and walls of the fort. John decided to divert there to collect some saltpeter, so that instead of having to make all of that substance, they would have a ready-made supply to start manufacture with.

They had found what they came for, and now the challenge was to get back home in one piece.

They returned to the oasis valley and set up camp not far from the city in the valley. John decided on a plan to send his raw materials home by the most concealed, shortest route. As a precaution, he figured that if there were any danger, it would come from the city nearby. So he organized a group of the soldiers and volunteers from the workers to scout the city. The plan was that if they saw any preparations for a possible attack on their party, they would attack first to produce a diversion that would draw the attackers away from the expedition.

John appointed one of the most able workers, Timothy, to be the leader. Timothy, who had dark hair and sharp features, had showed John that he had leadership qualities and could command the other men effectively. John advised Timothy to travel at night, if possible, and to stay away from the well-traveled road.

John took his contingent to the outskirts of the city. They waited till morning to observe the activity in the community. The city had a wall with battlements and gates. To the south and west of the city were the ruins of an ancient structure. From their vantage point on the hills to the west of the city, they could see a central plaza for shops. Small fortifications and barracks were in each of the six corners of the walls. A large building on the east side of the plaza appeared to be a house of worship. At each of the four corners of the building, there were towers with large, black semi-circles atop them. Several times a day, priests would come out of the towers and chant. When that occurred, everybody within the walls and outside the walls would stop and prostrate themselves to pray.

On the west side of the plaza was a large, turquoise, gold-domed building that looked like a palace. Just after noon each day, a group of prisoners was brought to the plaza to suffer beheading. Some of the prisoners would live, but their hands, ears, or other body parts were chopped off. Other prisoners were publicly whipped. John had no idea what their crimes were, but he did feel sorry for them. Because there did not appear to be any activity occurring in preparation for a raid, John decided to leave and catch up with the expedition.

About dusk, the following day, John reached the expedition, and they all reached the city by the fifteenth day after they had left. John immediately went to the palace and made a report to the archbishop about the expedition. The archbishop expressed great satisfaction that all members of the expedition had returned in good health. He, however, had greater interest in John's observations of the city to the east. John explained what he had observed and concluded that, at the present time, there didn't appear to be any preparations for war.

The archbishop then said, "The new religion is savage and persistent. When the time is right, the people will start preparing for war, for it is their aim to convert the whole world to their views, and they care not how much blood they shed."

John assured the archbishop that he would make all haste to develop the new protective weapons.

CHAPTER 9

Experiment and Invention

The next morning, John rushed to the commissioner's home to see Catherine. He was escorted into a large sitting area, where the commissioner and his family, including Catherine, were seated, eagerly anticipating his tales. Enthusiastically, John recounted the journey with all his observations, describing down to the minutest detail the eastern city. He was full of praise for the soldiers and the workman who had accompanied him. He especially praised Timothy, his right-hand man, as he called him.

After that, John and Catherine went for a walk in the garden. The moon was shining, and a gentle breeze was blowing. Catherine looked especially lovely that night. John couldn't help himself and began talking of plans that he had for both of them and of the great things he could do for the city and the faith.

Catherine seemed to be captivated by John's musings. John hoped that she was beginning to feel genuine attraction, even the beginnings of love for him. He resolved to remain a gentleman as he courted Catherine and never to be rude or forward.

As the evening went on, he and Catherine talked about their personal desires and dreams, the number of children in the ideal family, their favorite colors, foods, and relatives. The evening grew late, and Catherine's father reminded them of the hour. After thanking Catherine and her father for a wonderful evening, John gave Catherine a gentle kiss on the hand, a bow and said good night.

John awoke before the crowing of the roosters, got dressed, and hurried to the shop. If he was going to make gunpowder, he was going to have to recall basic high school chemistry and do a little experimenting. Timothy and the other workers arrived, unsure of what they were to do. John began to outline his plans to them. The first thing to do was to try to make gunpowder. If that could be done successfully, then the next item on the list was designs for simple hand grenades. And if those worked, John planned to design and produce more complicated devices.

John first wanted to evaluate the workmen's special skills, especially skills in making items of clay or ceramic, metal, glass, wood, and stone. He discovered that at least some of the workers were skilled in each of the required areas. John organized his shop into specialty areas and selected a worker as foreman of each area. He drew pictures and specifications for each item he wanted built. He had an idea of how these weapons operated from high school ROTC (Reserve Officer Training Corps).

John knew that making gunpowder would be dangerous, so he started with very small amounts and proceeded slowly. He first tried to mix equal amounts of saltpeter, sulfur, and charcoal. This did have some success, but it wasn't the most efficient, it burned incompletely. So he had to try different ratios of these ingredients. Some experimental ratios would not even burn. Eventually, he arrived at a ratio of ingredients that provided the best results. It seemed the best ratio had the highest proportion of saltpeter, which was the oxidant. The components had to be carefully and completely ground together, and were very, very dangerous. This hazard was reduced somewhat by adding water to the mixture. The slurry was passed through a mesh of coarsely woven cloth to make small pellets, which were allowed to dry.

The workers easily obtained charcoal from stores in the city. John sent some of his workers around to buy as much charcoal as they could find. He had to caution his workers continually about not having fire close in the vicinity of the gunpowder-making area of the shop. Occasionally there were small accidents, but no one was injured. When John had successfully produced enough gunpowder for experimentation, he had it stored in a specially constructed vault in the floor of the shop.

Next, John wanted to use the raw materials collected from the cave to produce potassium nitrate or saltpeter. He found a nearby cave outside the walls with a good dirt floor on which to place the guano. He mixed the guano with plant ashes. The alkalinity of the soil and the moisture in the cave in the warm climate, promoted nitrification, that is, conversion of nitrogen compounds from animal and plant decay into nitrates, which penetrated the soil. Deposits evaporated on the surface, forming crude saltpeter, a white, flowerlike powder, which had to be washed to remove the impurities and boiled to evaporate and refine it.

While John was busy producing and experimenting with the production of gunpowder, his other workers were busy at their tasks. The first devices were the hand grenades, which were to be made out of small, spherical clay pots with a fuse. John had a half-dozen experimental hand grenades constructed. He and Timothy took them outside the walls of the city to the valley that ran along the southeast side of the city. They found, first, that the grenades worked and second, that by varying the lengths of the fuses, they could cause detonation at different times. Of course, with all the noise, they attracted an audience from the city. It was this audience that made John decides to test the devices in a more secure and safer location.

He wanted to develop some type of artillery. He knew that catapults existed, as he had witnessed them firsthand. He didn't know if the people had trebuchets, which could throw grenades or shot made from stone or metal for long distances. A trebuchet was powered by a weight attached to one end of its throwing arm. John drew up a plan for a trebuchet and asked the woodworking section to build such a device.

Cannons were another matter. He did not know if this culture had the knowledge to produce cannons. The metalworking section said they knew of a man who had a bell foundry. John sent Timothy with the metalworkers to find this man and determine whether he would join them. In the meantime, John asked the stone working crew if they could fashion round, stone balls. He had to wait until he found out how big cannon could be produced before he could have cannonballs manufactured.

The next item he wanted to make was a telescope that would allow them to see the enemy earlier and farther away, and therefore be better prepared. He talked with the glassmaking section and described what he wanted. He asked them to produce circle-shaped glass of the specifications he indicated to fit a wooden tube.

Timothy returned from visiting the foundry man and said that the man wanted to meet John for discussion. Timothy led John to the foundry man's village southwest of the city. The small village had about a dozen rock houses and no wall. Several score of people lived in the village. A blacksmith shop was located next to the foundry, and both were located next to the stream that ran through the village.

As they approached the village, Timothy pointed out the man they had come to meet. He was near his foundry, talking with others, getting items, and taking them inside. The foundry man appeared to be middle-aged with grey hair and a potbelly, but he was still well-muscled and strong. His tunic was rough, and he wore a leather apron. He had a hint of grime on his brow, wore a short, grey beard, and had a well-tanned face and large, well-calloused hands. Upon reaching the foundry, Timothy knocked on the door. "Master Daniel, I have arrived with Master John. May we enter?"

Master Daniel replied in a gruff, heavy voice, "Please come in, and peace be with you."

John saw that the building had a furnace, bellows, and metal tools. Firewood and coke was stacked beside the wall next to the furnace. Master Daniel grasped John's hand in a vise-like grip and pumped it vigorously.

"Glad to meet you, Master John. I've heard a lot about you. Your men admire you, you know." He invited John to sit at a table in the corner of the work room, and the two men began discussing business.

"Sir, it's a pleasure meeting you," John said. "I understand that you have the expertise to make what I need—that is, what the city needs."

"I can make them," Daniel replied. "I've been doing this for years. My father was a foundry man, and his father was a foundry man before him. I have made many bronze and iron items of varying sizes over the years. Just describe what you want."

"What I want is . . . excuse me; do you have paper and a pen so I can draw it?"

"Yes, yes, of course." With the paper and pen before him, John began sketching a design and describing it as he drew.

An interested look came over Daniel as he looked at the sketch. "This presents a unique challenge, but I can make that. I've been making bells for years, and the largest ones have been three feet long and a foot and a half wide. To make a long tube with a smaller hole at one end leading to the larger bore is difficult, but not impossible. Do you want the tubes made of bronze or iron?"

"First make one of each so we can test them," John said. "When we decide which are the better cannon, then we will want to have a number made."

"By all means. Now let's talk payment."

"What do you require per cannon?"

Daniel wrote figures on John's sketch and showed the total to John, who smiled and wrote a second figure. Master Daniel examined the figure, looked at John, smiled, and wrote a third figure below the first two.

John looked up and smiled "Done, sir! And I will pay that price per cannon upon receiving the first two experimental ones. Then half of the remainder upon order of the rest and half upon receipt of them."

Their negotiations done, Master Daniel took John and Timothy on a short tour of his operation and explained how it worked. The material he used was mined in a desert about thirty leagues to the south. He bought the material from merchants who had bought it from the miners after it was smelted from the ore. Daniel had learned to melt the metal in a furnace, which was stoked by a bellows to make it hotter. He poured the hot metal into molds that he'd made from clay and sand. He could make steel items, but that was harder and the finished quality was somewhat haphazard.

At the end of the tour, Daniel invited John and Timothy to stay for dinner. The fare was simple but plentiful. They toasted the conclusion of the meeting with wine—all except Timothy— and stayed until the next day, when they left at dawn after bidding all farewell.

CHAPTER 10

Sermon

With his work well begun, John would go to the shop to work during the day or leave on small expeditions for several days at a time. At night, however, John would spend as much time as possible with Catherine. They would attend street shows, the theater, and public functions together and would eat at local establishments. John showered her with gifts and made a point to give gifts to her family as well. Sometimes they went to her father's house and spent time together in the garden. It was at these times that John reminisced about his previous life to her. Their relationship was growing day by day, and John believed that both of them were falling more and more in love with each other.

During one of these times in the garden, under the moonlight, surrounded by flowers John proposed marriage to Catherine. He bent down on one knee and spoke with a little tremble in his voice that betrayed both excitement and fear of the possible outcome.

"Catherine, I love you so much. You have given me hope and love that I thought I could never have. I promise to take care of you and give you love. I have much to learn about your world, as I know I am a stranger here, so please have patience with me. I want . . . no, I need to share my life with you. Will you marry me?"

She paused for a moment and then, with a warm smile and a nod, replied, "Every time I am with you, my heart fills with happiness. I feel safe, and you are what I have hoped for. Yes, John, of course

I will marry you!" They embraced and shared a long, passionate kiss.

They decided to wait until the perfect time for the ceremony. But they went back into the house to announce the engagement to her parents. The commissioner and his wife said that they were happy and proud to have a man such as John ask to marry their daughter. With his talents, they knew he would go far.

When John was not busy with the shop, Catherine's father would ask him to accompany him to community meetings. This way, John started learning how the city government operated. He would sometimes help the commissioner collect the licensing fees from the merchants. He would also help him with the mathematics involved in the accounting of his office. The commissioner had a small panel of bureaucrats to handle the day-to-day affairs of the office. Hearing John deliver instructions to these bureaucrats on his behalf, the commissioner said he was very pleased and noted that John's charismatic baritone voice would stand him in good stead as a community leader.

John attended church every Sunday in the large city basilica, Saint Stephens, with the commissioner and his family. Situated close to the palace, the basilica was built of white marble with Doric columns in front of the large, plain bronze doors. A large, golden dome dominated its superstructure, and a single flight of fifteen steps extended the length of the portico. Flanking the steps were two large statues of angels. Inside, an atrium led into the vaulted nave containing row upon row of benches between the pillars. The altar was a large, gilded table which held a chalice, two candlesticks at each end, and a large, gold cross in the center. Underneath the altar was a vault said to contain the bones of Saint Stephen, the first Christian martyr. On the ceiling of the apse was a fresco of Christ performing the sign of the blessing. On either side of the altar were large, cushioned chairs for the bishops, archbishop, and priests. An ornate pulpit stood out from the chairs on the right.

The archbishop would occasionally give a sermon in the basilica. Most of the time the priests of the church would do the preaching. The sermons usually focused on fire and brimstone, promising salvation and the glories of Paradise or the damnation and punishment of hell. The sermons included lessons on how to behave. Occasionally, a male layman from the congregation was invited to give a sermon or a talk—provided it was consistent with church beliefs. There was no question of who was the authority in the church, the commissioner told John, but giving occasional sermons afforded the people the feeling of participating and contributing. It was with this opening that the commissioner asked the church authorities to invite John to give a sermon.

John felt honored to be asked to give a sermon in so grand a basilica. But he wasn't sure what to talk about. He agonized over the topic for two weeks. Then he had an idea: Why not talk about God's wonderful creation—the world, the universe? He spent many hours thinking about what he was going to say and how he was going to say it. He felt that he was almost back in seminary and having to compose his first sermon, one that would be graded and critiqued. In this case, the critique would be made by the priests, and John's words would be graded by the archbishop himself.

On the Sunday that he was to give the sermon, instead of going in the grand front entrance, he went in a side entrance. He was escorted into a room for the priests to dress themselves. Many elaborate robes, headwear, and other accoutrements were stored in that room. Each priest had two boys who aided him in dressing himself appropriately. When it was time, they proceeded in a line out to the altar, where they bowed and crossed themselves before sitting. John felt very anxious as the priests made the usual introductions and opening remarks. He could feel butterflies fluttering in his stomach. When he was introduced, he rose and strode to the pulpit, hoping that he looked confident, though he really wasn't.

He began, "My Christian brothers and sisters, it is with great humility that I speak to you today. The city and this faith have given me great hope for the future. And it is with this same faith and hope in our Lord Jesus Christ that I share my vision of our world and our universe. Jesus came to save all the peoples of the world, as we are all children of the Father and Creator. The wonder and mystery of life now and in the hereafter are what join us all. From the smallest seed to the largest mountain, God has granted us dominion. We as children of God, and by the grace of God, have been granted the ability to manipulate what we see around us for the glory of God and of His Son. Indeed, we must use that power to build and establish a paradise, a kingdom of God. And in doing so, we will be helping all of God's children. This includes bringing salvation and God's word to others. It is our duty to bring the world to Christ's dominion."

The congregation, the priests, and indeed, the archbishop himself seemed duly impressed with John's sermon by their smiles and head nodding. The Commissioner commented to gentleman seated next to him that he was both eloquent and charismatic in his oratory. He continued speaking for about twenty minutes more, and, as Catherine told him later, he captivated all that heard. What he had to say was, he hoped, different from the usual fire-and-brimstone sermon.

The archbishop thanked John for speaking and said that he was indeed talented in many areas, adding that the church might have great use of him in the future.

At the end of the service, John returned to the robbing room and, with the help of the boys, took off his ecclesiastical garments. The archbishop, the priests, and several prominent citizens came back to the room and congratulated him on delivering such a stirring sermon. Leaving the basilica, John felt that he had accomplished something important.

CHAPTER 11

Artillery

Over the next several months, John's work at his shop continued. He suffered many trials and numerous errors before he experienced success with each section of the work. The workmen finally figured out how to produce the saltpeter in quantity from the cave. Once that was done, they could produce the propellant in quantity.

John secured permission to store the gunpowder in an ancient quarry. He also secured a site, not far from the city, where he and his men could experiment and test the new inventions. The catapults and trebuchets worked very well. The men could launch stones or the hand grenades with these devices. They expended effort and time in determining the ranges at which each device was most effective.

One day, the foundry man delivered two cannons, one of bronze and one of iron. Over the next thirty days, they experimented with gradually increasing charges of powder. John wanted to find the bursting point for each cannon. Testing determined that bronze was not the most suitable material to use for cannons. From then on, he ordered only iron cannons.

John determined that the number cannons to be ordered would be equivalent to the number of gates in the wall and the number of towers. The number of trebuchets would be equivalent to the number of barracks positions along each wall. John imported some of the finest cedar from the land to the northwest of the city. He planned to use the timber to build the carriages for the guns and the trebuchets.

Finished with the experimentation and development of John's inventions, his workers became more proficient in their operation. Several of the workmen who were highly skilled at operating the guns and the trebuchets became instructors for the city's soldiers, who later would man the weapons.

With those operations proceeding smoothly in the shop, John concentrated on developing a telescope. Glass had been made for centuries but had not been used in any type of optics. He undertook lengthy experiments in grinding the lenses. The difficulty that stopped him most of the time was fine-polishing the lenses. Finally he thought of asking Catherine for some of her rouge, and that was the breakthrough. John remembered from college that often lens and mirrors could be polished to great accuracy using rouge, a very fine powder. The lenses came out polished well enough to be used in a telescope. John's lenses had some slight imperfections which nevertheless did not sufficiently distort the image to make the telescope unusable. His first telescope could magnify distant objects two to three times. Later, he developed telescopes that could magnify up to ten times.

CHAPTER 12

Opening Shots

The trouble first began with occasional reports from outlying villages that foreign soldiers were gathering in the east. John was still several months from finishing his preparations for mounting the guns and trebuchets. Scouts were dispatched to the east and were ordered to return with intelligence. In the meantime, the tension in the city started to increase. The archbishop ordered the citizens to begin gathering supplies within the city walls. He also asked John to finish his preparations as expeditiously as possible. And the archbishop asked the commissioners, military commanders, John, and other leaders and officials of the city to attend a conference chaired by the archbishop himself.

The group met in the great throne room of the palace. A crude map lay on a table in front of the throne, and the leaders and officials gathered around it. General Alexander wore armor that combined well-polished Roman and medieval plate armor with a scarlet cape. He was clean shaven, and his hair was half brown and half grey. He carried an air of authority and command.

Archbishop Gregory said, "General Alexander, would you please brief the assembled leaders and dignitaries as to the present situation?"

A hush permeated the room. "Gentlemen," the general said in a somber tone, "we are facing a situation similar to others in the past, but of far greater threat. The outcome may affect the survival of the city and the faith. The eastern city has gathered a huge army, and apparently they mean to conquer us."

The general paused for a moment and looked sternly around the room. "It is up to us to stop them. My aide is distributing a paper describing the enemy's numbers, machines of war, and supplies. We must prepare our city for war and siege. These preparations are occurring as I speak. Every able-bodied man must be ready to fight. Every leader here must see to the preparation of his section and organization. We have set out messengers to every Christian village and city in the area to prepare similarly and to send us any surplus warriors or to move their populations here."

Pointing to the map, the general outlined the current enemy position, allied cities and villages, and the strategy for the city's defense.

Following the conference, all the attendees returned first to their homes to prepare their families. John and the commissioner talked as they were returning to their respective residences as to what preparations they should make. John wanted to see Catherine before he lost himself in the business of war. When he had concluded his own home preparations, he visited Catherine at the commissioner's house

Upon seeing John, Catherine exclaimed, "Oh John, how I love you!" They rushed into each other's arms and embraced. He could see that she was quite afraid.

"It will be all right, darling," he said. "We are safe behind these city walls, and the general has a good defense plan."

Catherine grew calmer but still said, "If the city falls, we will never be able to have a life together. I hear that the enemy army is huge and has new weapons—and they are not kind to those they conquer. I've heard that slavery, death, or even worse is what happens to those that stand in their way. Please, please, please, John don't let them take me alive." She began to sob.

John held her and stroked her hair. Then he put his hand under her chin and lifted her eyes to his. "Sweetheart, I will not let anything happen to you, and I want you to trust me. God will not allow the city to fall. I know we will win, especially with my new weapons. Please don't cry. Do you trust me?"

"Yes, yes, I do, my love."

"I want you to stay here, for there is no safer place in the city. Be strong, and we'll get through this together. I must go now, but I will be back." Catherine tried to smile. She kissed John once more before he left.

Rushing back to his shop, John saw much activity in the streets. Civilians were rushing about, gathering last-minute supplies, and securing their homes. The men with their personal weapons were gathering at mustering centers. He arrived at his shop where he found Timothy and the others donning armor and taking up weapons. John led his small contingent to the nearest mustering center. Upon arrival, the officer in charge of the center recognized John as the inventor of the new weapons. He told John to report with his men directly to the palace and General Alexander.

John and his men found the general in front of the palace in the plaza. The general said that because John and his men were so valuable, they would not be used as warriors but as advisors. John and Timothy would remain with the general, and the others would be strategically stationed around the walls to help with the new weapons.

John stood on the northeast corner of the wall with Archbishop Gregory, General Alexander, and the staff. John was able to point out the approach of the enemy, which he could see clearly through his telescope. As the enemy force got closer, they became more recognizable. Banners were flying in front of the column of soldiers, some of whom wore brightly colored uniforms. Some soldiers wore armor, while others had only shields with which to defend themselves. The enemy carried a mix of spears, swords, and crossbows. One unit was armed with an ancient weapon, leather slings, and pouches of stones.

An enemy cavalry unit armed with lances and shields began to deploy in a long line on top of the hill across the valley from the city. Word soon arrived that another cavalry unit was approaching from the southeast. It soon became apparent that the two units were attempting surround the city. Behind the line of cavalry appeared the major weapons. John could identify catapults, battering rams, siege towers, and trebuchets!

Coming down from the hill was a grandly robed individual, the enemy general with his aides, all on white horses. Under a flag of truce, they crossed the valley and approached the most northeasterly gate of the city. The archbishop and General Alexander went to that gate's battlement with their own flag of truce to parlay with their opposite numbers.

The foreign general began, "May it please you, our Grand Leader, who is the direct descendent of the prophet, desires not to take your blood. Too much blood has been spilled between us over the centuries. He desires only that you surrender the city to us. Then all in the city will be spared."

General Alexander replied, "And if we do this, what will happen to those who are spared?"

The answer was swift and assured. "They will become followers of the one true religion, the one true prophet, the one true God. Theirs will be paradise and life."

General Alexander asked, "For those who do not convert but remain loyal to their faith, what will be their fate?"

"Those who ignore God's revelations shall be sternly punished. They shall become fuel for the fire."

General Alexander said sternly, "We can never deny Christ and the true faith of our Lord. Therefore, let it be war!"

John looked on in disbelief. There had been no attempt at negotiation or compromise. Indeed, he thought, we must not surrender the city or ourselves. God is on our side, and with the help of Jesus Christ, the enemy army will be smashed.

The general asked John, "When should we use the new weapons?"

"Not yet . . . not yet."

"When, then?" The general sounded impatient.

"When the time is right," John said, "and I shall indicate it to you."

The enemy was advancing on all fronts: up the steep valley of the northeast, through the valley on the southeast, and from the plane southwest to the northwest. When the enemy soldiers were a few hundred yards from the walls, they began using their trebuchets and catapults. About seventy-five yards out, the archers began their barrage, and the crossbowmen concentrated on the tower defenders. Closer to the walls, slingers started their barrage of projectiles to provide cover so that the battering rams and siege towers could to be moved up.

On the city's walls, the archers began returning fire at the approaching enemy infantry. John ordered the trebuchets to begin returning fire. The number of enemy and defender bodies began to increase. Soon, the siege towers were pushed over the bodies of the dead and dying. John heard horrible screams from all around the city. Enemy warriors who were advancing on the city walls would slip on their comrades' blood.

As the siege towers approached the gate battlements, John ordered the cannons to fire. The siege towers were torn apart by the cannonade. Pieces of siege tower and body parts were blown about and rained down upon the troops.

John had ordered the hand grenades to be stored all along the city battlements. When the enemy warriors were at the base of the walls and attempting to scale them by ladder and grappling hooks, John then told the general to give the signal to use the hand grenades. The resulting gore and destruction was tremendous, so much so that the enemy commander ordered a retreat to the nearby hills.

A cheer went up from the defenders on the walls. John could see that his weapons had performed as he had declared they could. He was proud of his men and of the weapons they had produced under his leadership. However, he could see that the enemy was not done. In the distance, he could see that they were making camp, no doubt to return as soon as they could.

That night, funeral pyres glowed across the distant line of hills. The wounded of the city were taken to the hospital. The bodies of the city's defenders who had been killed outright were burned in pyres. Inside the city, the general called a council of war immediately after the services for the dead. John was specifically invited and was given a golden medallion by Archbishop Gregory for the spectacular performance of the weapons in repelling the first attack. The assembled leaders assessed what materials and defenses they had remaining. The city had adequate stocks of food and water. Water supply was accessible through large cisterns throughout the city and through an ancient tunnel that led to an underground spring. The supply of ammunition in the form of projectiles, arrows, and gunpowder was plentiful enough to last for months. The defense's weak points were determined to be the gates themselves. Therefore, the leaders decided to build reinforcing walls behind the gates.

CHAPTER 13

Rescue Mission

The city's spies reported the enemy's decision to blockade the city. John continued watching the enemy through his telescope. The enemy soldiers appeared to be thoroughly covering the neighboring countryside to gather supplies and intelligence. Through his telescope, John could observe their camps and their ceremonies. He could also see what happened to innocent citizens who were caught outside the city walls. The enemy crucified them within sight of the city and laughed at their pitiful screams as the nails were driven through the victims' flesh. As they died over many days, their moans gradually grew silent. The sight was hideous.

John inquired as to the whereabouts of Daniel, but evidently the foundry man was not in the city. If he were caught, the enemy would then have the knowledge to make cannons and defend against them. Whether they could force Daniel to help them was questionable—but if the enemy was successful in obtaining and using Daniels's knowledge, John knew that the walls of the city could not stand such a bombardment. He went to the general with his concerns, asking to mount a rescue mission if he could determine Daniel's location.

A rescue team consisting of John, Timothy, and a squad of soldiers was organized. John decided that they would leave the city at night through an ancient tunnel that opened under the city's east wall. From there, they moved along the east wall and around the south wall. They used boulders and brush for cover as they made their way along. At the southwest corner, they used a shallow gulley to get past the enemy lines. Occasionally, they would have to stop and wait for a sentry to reverse his line of march.

After they were well past the enemy lines, they used the remaining hours of the night to move rapidly. By dawn, they were several miles away from the city and the blockading army.

They made their way to the village of the foundry man and found that it had been pillaged. They found no sign of him or any other living people. In fact, the village was deserted except for some dogs eating the remains of four gruesomely mutilated and unrecognizable bodies. So they began to search the nearby countryside, checking each cave and other possible hiding place they came upon. After two days, they found Daniel, cowering in a small cave halfway up a hill near a dry river bed. He was cold and hungry and seemed quite frightened. After they gave him some bread and water, he told them what had happened to his village.

"After the messenger arrived at our village from the city," Daniel said in a quavering voice, "he encouraged us to move our possessions and families to the city, and most people did so quickly. A few of us decided to stay and hide what we could, destroying the rest of our goods. I was just returning from the place where I hid the plans for your guns, John. As I crossed the crest of a hill, I could see the barbarians filling the village. Four of my comrades had been captured and were on their knees before the commander of the raiding party, being interrogated for information."

Daniel's voice broke, and tears started to form in his eyes. "My comrades refused to speak or tell them anything! They did not betray my position or my occupation or what I did for you. These were truly brave men. The barbarians demanded that my comrades convert and worship their god and prophet. But my men told their captors that if they did so, their souls would burn in hell. The captors responded that if they did not accept the barbarian faith, they would still burn in hell. Because my comrades still refused, one by one they were filleted alive. I could do nothing to help them. Oh, God forgive me!"

John tried to comfort him as best he could. "Daniel, you're safe now. We are here to take you back to the city. Was Thomas one of the men killed?"

Daniel nodded in the affirmative.

"Thomas and the others are with our Lord now," John said. "Be comforted in that. A time will come when his death and the other deaths will be avenged. We'll stay here for a little while and rest. But we must move tonight and get back to the city. We cannot do it in daylight, as we'll be spotted. Daniel, will you come with us?"

With vengeance in his voice, Daniel said, "Of course, John. Give me a moment to collect myself. I want to contribute in any way I can to the destruction of those heathen who murdered my friends."

John determined to wait until dark to return to the city. He and his men decided to stay below the crest of the hills and not follow a straight-line route. Because of the geography of the wilderness, one could get lost in the daytime as well as at night. During the journey home, they made several wrong turns and had to backtrack several times. But eventually they made their way to the rear of the enemy lines, which they had to pass somehow.

Sentries were posted thickly, and at intervals the armed guards marching between the sentries. John's group would have to wait until a guard started marching away from them and try to slip through to the cover of the boulders and brush surrounding the wall. The timing would have to be perfect.

John decided to send Daniel and three of the soldiers through first. He ordered them to head for the entrance to the tunnel, no matter what happened. The next group would be Timothy and three more soldiers. John would lead the last group of soldiers and bring up the rear. Daniel's and Timothy's groups got through quickly. As John's group was passing through the sentry line, he thought he heard one of his soldiers slip on the rocky soil, producing enough noise that a sentry spotted them. They tried to run for it, but got only a short distance. John's soldiers put up a violent and valiant defense, fighting not only to defend themselves, but to defend their city's honor. Their efforts were to no avail, and they were killed. John was cornered by a half dozen enemy soldiers, and as he had no weapons, he surrendered.

CHAPTER 14

Captured

John was taken to the sentry commander's tent and presented as a prize. The commander ordered that John be immediately executed, but then one of the company officers recognized John as the man who had invented and developed the secret weapons of the city. His execution stayed, John was taken to the general of the enemy army for questioning. His hands were tied behind his back, and a noose placed around his neck was used as a leash.

He was led into a large, colorful tent. Carpets were placed on the ground inside, and large, elaborately detailed pillows were arranged as seats. The general was seated on one of them.

The commander of the guard presented John. "Your Excellency, it is my duty and honor to present to you Master John Pope."

The general approached John, circled him twice, and spoke. "I suppose you were wondering how we know about you," he said. "We have spies in the city, just as the city has spies in our city and villages. We have been aware of your work. We even know of your journey to the salt sea. We didn't know how effective your weapons would be. I congratulate you on your successful work."

John said, "If you knew my work, then why didn't your spies provide information on how to make your own weapons or defend against them?"

The general frowned and said, "We only knew of the work, and the information was terminated prematurely when one of our spies was captured and executed. He was not able to send enough information for us to develop countermeasures. Meanwhile, the other spy has not been able to get any information out to us."

John was astonished. Another spy, he thought! "Who is he?"

The general, looking amused, said, "It would do no good as the other is of no consequence now. We have you."

The general graciously offered John a cup of strong tea and asked, "Would you join us now?"

John considered his options. "If I do not, what will be my fate?"

"Death."

"What must I do to save my life?"

Without hesitation, the general said, "You must first accept the one true God and his prophet, and then you must help us."

I have to buy time, John thought. "May I have time to think about it?" he asked.

"Yes, you may have a little time," said the general. "And I will also provide you with some instruction on our faith." John's bonds were cut, and he was taken to a tent of his own, but he was kept under heavy guard.

A cleric was assigned to teach him about their religion for six hours each day. John learned that their prophet had been born approximately fourteen hundred years ago. The prophet was given revelations from God, and the revelations were codified into their holy text. Originally, the faith began as a cult, much as Christianity did, and later developed into a full religion. Like Christianity and Judaism, the new faith was concerned with moral behavior and social justice. The one true God was the same God that Christians and Jews worshiped.

At one time, there was considerable exchange of ideas among the three religions, as all the believers were the descendents of Abraham. But at some point, believers splintered the faith into distinct subgroups and rivalries occurred as each group competed for the faithful. New ideas were added from other cultures, along with some old traditions and paranoia, eventually a new form of Islam began to evolve. This new way of looking at the world threatened the position of the various religious leaders. So a more intolerant and virulent view emerged, not taught by the prophet. Their goal was to spread Islam worldwide.

At that point, John realized that this new religion was what he knew as Islam. He also realized that there would be no compromising with these believers and that he wouldn't be tolerated if he didn't convert. He began to search for an escape.

At night, the guards were doubled around his tent. During the day, between lessons, he was allowed to walk around the camp under guard. He saw how the Muslim army was organized and made mental notes of what he saw, including the types of siege weapons. One of those weapons was the ballista, a Roman adaptation of a Greek weapon. A ballista was essentially a large crossbow, very powerful, accurate, and effective at long distances. It could fire large arrows called bolts or stone shot.

John was given two meals a day. The only time he was alone was when he had to relieve himself. Everybody went to his own favorite spot, somewhat concealed, and performed his bodily functions. But during the day, it was still much too dangerous for him to attempt to escape.

So one night, John asked one of his guards if he could go relieve himself. The guard said he could, but he would have to accompany John. This was John's chance. He found a little ravine with some large boulders on the side of the hill opposite the encampment. The guard was bigger than he was and was armored, so John knew that he could not disable and quiet him by force. When the guard was turned away from him to give John privacy, he crept behind a boulder and sneaked down the hill. He quickly followed a gulley around the hill to below the walls of the city. Using the cover of the boulders and brush at the base of the walls, he raced to the secret entrance of the tunnel under the east wall. There John was ecstatic to see Timothy and the other soldiers, who had apparently waited for days in the tunnel for John to return. Timothy told John that they'd had faith John would escape and return to them.

CHAPTER 15

Betrayed

Immediately upon his return, John was escorted to General Alexander and Archbishop Gregory, who gave him a close interrogation, asking about the enemy strength, their composition, their strategy, and last, what they had wanted of him. The questioning took several hours, and by early morning, they were finished and allowed John to go home and rest. He awoke early in the afternoon of the following day, dressed quickly, and went first to see Catherine and then to examine his shop. Catherine was relieved that he was safe. He told her briefly of the escape, and then he had to leave. Upon arrival at his shop, he found all in an uproar. He learned that Timothy had been arrested and had been taken to the dungeon at the palace.

"Why?" John asked, shocked.

A workman replied, "I don't know. A squad of soldiers arrived this morning and arrested him without mentioning the charges."

Timothy was John's right-hand man and his most faithful worker. John hurried to the palace to confront General Alexander. He found the general at work in his office.

Bursting into the room, John cried, "Why has Timothy been arrested?"

The general was startled and told the others in the room to excuse themselves, as he wished to have a private conversation with John. When the last person left, the General said, "Timothy was arrested on suspicion of treason and espionage."

When John was seated comfortably, the general explained. "We've had our suspicions, which you confirmed last night. When you told us that the enemy general had spies in our city, we knew that we had to take action based on our suspicions. Why do you think we sent a squad of soldiers with you on that rescue mission? It would have been far simpler and safer to send a smaller number of men. However, when you requested that Timothy go along, we needed security. The soldiers had orders to kill him if he made any attempt to contact the enemy. Fortunately, he did not make such an attempt. However, when the soldiers returned without you, we were alarmed and suspicious. The soldier that you supposedly heard slip as you were trying to get out was not slipping by accident. It was Timothy, who made noise to reveal your position to the enemy. This was the report we received from the soldiers accompanying Timothy back to the city. They couldn't reveal themselves, but they did come to us with the truth."

John sank his head in his hands as the general continued. "After that, Timothy was never left alone. He always had an escort of soldiers. When you left the tunnel with Timothy and the soldiers, another squad of our soldiers reentered the tunnel. They went to the exit and saw a contingent of enemy soldiers approaching the entrance to the tunnel. With the help of some of your other workers, we'd had a device made beforehand to blow up the tunnel and block the entrance, if needed. And we were forced to use that device."

The general placed his hand gently on John's shoulder. "John, how could the enemy soldiers know the precise location of the tunnel's entrance? We believe that Timothy, if that's his real name, left a small map for the enemy to find in the village of the foundry man.

"By the way, the foundry man himself is doing well and is busily contributing to the defense of our city. Thanks to the efforts of our spies, we have also rounded up other suspicious individuals who were evidently helping Timothy in his espionage work."

John couldn't say anything for a period of many minutes. Tears welled up in his eyes, and at last he asked, "May I see Timothy?"

"Of course," the general said. "I will have you escorted to his cell."

John was led down a long, stone staircase into the bowels of the palace. The place was dark and dank with a foul, moldy odor. The only light came from torches on the walls. When John and his escort reached the bottom of the staircase, he saw a large room with several men chained to the wall. One man being whipped with a flagellum was screaming in anguish, rivulets of blood dripping down his back. Another man was being tortured on the rack.

John was led back to a long tunnel that opened up into a room with individual cells. Large, heavy wooden doors with large straps of iron bolted across them provided barriers to escape. He was led to the third cell on the right, and the door was opened. Sitting on the floor and chained tightly to the wall was Timothy. His bed was now only a pallet of filthy straw, and Timothy was bloodied and bruised from the tortures he had received.

John's feelings of anger, remorse, and compassion welled up inside him. He asked, "Why?"

Timothy slowly responded, "You are a good man and a brilliant one. But your inventions and devices could spell the end of my master. I am not afraid to die, as I will be a martyr and go directly to heaven. Many rewards await me there. My master assured me that he would spare you if you were caught. Your inventions would have allowed us to conquer the world, and then a truly Islamic society could have been built as Allah's paradise on earth."

John felt anger replace his other emotions. "I confided in you, Timothy! I trusted you like a son!"

Timothy hung his head and said, "For that, I will always be deeply grateful to Allah."

John left the dungeon furious but heartbroken. Two days later, Timothy and half dozen others were publicly hanged.

CHAPTER 16

The Battle

After Timothy's execution, John became depressed and melancholy. He spent several days with Catherine, who tried with some success to cheer him up. She walked in her father's garden with John and took long strolls in the city to visit popular sites. During this time with her, John reflected sadly on what he had seen and done. After many days, he confided in Catherine.

"I don't understand why Timothy did that to me. Was his faith in his prophet and God stronger than mine? Is that why he became a spy? He must have known he could be captured and killed. He was my right-hand man, and I thought of him as a brother or son. Why did he do it?"

He stopped speaking and looked far away— farther away than the next wall or room or building or city gate. He was looking into his soul. At last he said, "Was it for honor, for glory, for God that he did those things? Was it for the salvation of his enemies and himself? If God loves his people, then He must be ashamed that we destroy one another in his name for our own version of religion."

John talked on and on, examining himself and trying to understand Timothy, and Catherine listened, nodded her head, smiled, and offered encouraging words.

"John," she said, "we do not know why God allows such evil. He must have a plan of some kind. If he doesn't or if there is no God, then what we do to each other appears senseless."

John smiled sadly and said, "Yes, it means that man is no better than the other beasts. Man kills for empty ideas based on religious doctrines. We kill and threaten only to impose our will on others. And it has nothing whatsoever to do with God! Catherine, if we survive this war, we must do something to change the way men behave . . . but what? Maybe . . . maybe we should. . . ." Again John became lost in reflection.

Catherine waited for awhile and then held him close, saying, "Yes, my love, yes."

As time passed with no resumption of the fighting, John felt his mood improve. Without Catherine's loving support, he would have had greater difficulty in moving out of melancholy rumination. He began going back to the shop, where the workers reintroduced him to the tasks at hand.

John started working on a design for a microscope, one a little more complicated than the first microscope that Antony van Leeuwenhoek developed in the late 1600s. While he was busy refining his design, a summons from the palace arrived, informing John that he was to attend General Alexander at his headquarters forthwith. There the general told John that the enemy was massing for a new attack and that the enemy was building new siege towers of a different design. He asked John whether any other preparations should be made before battle.

John wasn't sure of the answer and asked the general for more time to consider the question.

"Sir," the general replied, "you'd better think quickly because the enemy will not grant us much time."

John took his telescope up to the battlements to view what he could of the developments in the enemy camp. What he spied appeared to be the construction of two large siege towers without crossing bridges. Thick planks of cedar and oak were being affixed to the towers' fronts. A platform at the level of the gate battlements was constructed for some purpose, but not for that of conveying troops across. At the base large battering rams were being constructed as integral parts of the tower. In the front planking, at the level of the platform, was a large, open slit that was obviously designed for projectiles to pass through. But what kind of projectiles, John asked himself.

Stephen Stripe & Kevin Stripe

He returned to the general's command post and told him that he believed the enemy would attack not with one or two towers only, but in force. John also informed him that he was going to make some modifications to the city's gate tower cannons.

He had time to finish modifications to only three of the gate tower cannons before the enemy began its approach. General Alexander insisted that John stay throughout the battle at the general's side as an advisor and witness the battle from the city battlements.

Clouds hung low over the region and had an eerie red tint from the many campfires in and around the city. Cavalry units moved around the city to make a feint at the west wall, and one of the modified siege towers began approaching the northwest gate tower. The other modified siege tower approached the southwest gate tower. The enemy's other; older siege towers that were still intact from the previous attack approached the east wall gate towers. Most of the enemy force was behind the southwest siege tower.

John had been able to modify only the tower cannons on the northwest gate, the northeast gate, and the southeast gate. These modifications were a combination of wood and iron that made up a shield that protected the gunners.

All around the city's perimeter, the enemy positioned their trebuchets and catapults. At a prearranged signal, the trebuchets started firing. Next, the shorter-ranged catapults began firing. The projectiles consisted of stone, a type of Greek fire, and bodies of the executed Christians. When the siege towers were within range, the general ordered the gate tower cannon to fire. The older siege towers were devoid of troops, but were destroyed anyway. The two modified siege towers had ballistae firing through the slits. The bolts from the ballistae ricocheted off the northwest gate tower shield or stuck into it. The stone cannon shot ricocheted or broke up after hitting the siege tower's fortified face planking. When that happened, the gun crew switched to iron shot, which did penetrate and do damage. However, the southwest siege tower ballista operators had no trouble in hitting the unprotected gate tower gunners and thus allowed the siege tower to move close to the gate.

General Alexander moved his reserve troops of the sixth legion to the southwest gate tower to form a line of defense in case the wall was breached. He left enough troops manning the walls and the other gate towers to provide an effective defense. He had a contingent of cavalry, each man armed with a longer sword called a spatha, positioned in the plaza of the basilica to use as a rapid reserve or to exploit an opportunity. The palace or Templar guard was also kept in reserve at the same location.

The archers could not effectively disable the men operating the battering ram because of the modified sidewalls of the siege tower. The enemy troops came up behind the tower, using their shields in the Roman testudo, or tortoise, formation. The soldiers made the testudo formation by overlapping rectangular shields around themselves and over their heads, forming a box to protect them from projectiles. The men manning the walls began throwing the hand grenades at the siege tower and the enemy troops. They were somewhat effective against the testudo but useless against the siege tower. The battering ram was so huge that it didn't take long for the gates to be shattered and the hastily built defensive wall behind the gates was not substantial enough to withstand the ram.

When the gate wall collapsed, enemy soldiers rushed into the city and start forming a line of battle. John watched in fascination as the men of the sixth legion made a saw formation four ranks deep in the streets. The saw formation was a Roman defensive formation that placed one or more ranks of soldiers behind the main ranks. The secondary ranks moved back and forth to reinforce any faltering parts of the main line.

The city's soldiers began hurling their pilia as soon as the enemy troops gained access to the city. The enemy troops also threw their spears. The citizens in the streets started panicking and ran deeper into the city. They were already trying to put out the fires from the bombs launched from the enemy trebuchets. John could hear screams everywhere. Several hundred enemy troops were able to form a line several ranks deep within the city.

City soldiers on the gates and on the walls threw hand grenades, rocks, and spears at the invaders and shot arrows into the mass of enemy soldiers. At first, by sheer pressure of numbers, the invading soldiers were able to push the city's sixth legion back for more than a hundred yards.

Standing beside the general, John witnessed the battle from the city ramparts on the city's south wall. He said, "General, if we could get the gunners to fire long volleys at the enemy troops marching toward the southwest gate, and if we can have the trebuchets firing at the same area, then the enemy's reinforcements could be broken. If we can do that, the attackers who are now within the walls would fail and be forced to retreat. I say we forget the siege tower and the ballista, for they are having no effect now."

General Alexander responded an order, "Captain, send messengers to the gun and trebuchets crews to change their angle of fire. They are to concentrate on the reinforcements coming into the city from the enemy camp. Also, send a message to the Templar commander. I want his troops moved up to reinforce the sixth legion. When the bombardment commences, change formations, and push the barbarians out of our city. Hurry, captain, for this must be done quickly if we are to win the day."

With that order, the artillery angled their shots toward the enemy reinforcement column. Cannonballs and projectiles of all kinds began taking their toll. The trebuchets also loosed flaming pitch onto the invading troops. The enemy who were marching toward the gate to add to their comrades' strength failed to reach them. Further, the tortoise formation was ineffective against cannon shot and trebuchet projectiles, which dismembered soldiers on impact. Many of the enemy became torches, running into others and causing confusion.

When the reinforcement formations broke up, the individual members were hit with arrows and slings. Then the sixth legion, supported by reinforcements from the Templar guard, changed to the wedge formation and pushed the enemy back to the walls. Sword and battle-ax cleaved and hacked a bloody path that day, and John watched as enemy arms, legs, and heads were separated from their torsos. Those that were not killed outright were trampled to death by those marching over them.

Heroes emerged on both sides during the fighting. Some of them would survive, but most would not. With enemy reinforcements taking casualties from the rear and with front line troops taking casualties from the sixth legion and the walls, the invading attackers finally collapsed and ran, chased by troops from the sixth legion.

At that point, General Alexander unleashed his cavalry to conduct slaughter in its bloodiest detail. John saw men cut down from behind, while some turned and faced their destiny. Lance, sword, battle-ax, and mace all took their portion of life and death. The cavalry ran down men in their haste to take the enemy encampment. Pursuing horses and men slipped on the blood that flowed down the road from the enemy camp.

The enemy general and his staff fled east. A good proportion of his army escaped with him, minus their siege weapons. General Alexander's men wanted to chase the enemy all the way to the salt sea. But the general knew that he had suffered many casualties as well and did not have the manpower, weapons, or supplies to kill every enemy soldier. The city's soldiers contented themselves by racing to the enemy camp, where they massacred every opponent still left there. General Alexander and John followed on horseback, with a squad of mounted Templars as bodyguards, to see for themselves. The enemy camp was a shambles. The dead lay everywhere. Body parts were severed partially or entirely. The engines of war were either burning or being dismantled by the triumphant city soldiers. All that was left of the tents were burnt pieces of cloth and charred tent poles.

John observed some of the city soldiers taking trophies of armor and weapons from the dead. Some soldiers even cut enemy fingers off to claim a ring as a prize. The holy relics carried by the enemy were desecrated and destroyed. John was horrified and sickened by what he was seeing. These were not the honorable soldiers of God and Christ but a pack of vengeful, inhuman animals.

At John's urging, General Alexander ordered the chaos and violent behavior to cease. It was a great victory— but at what a cost!

CHAPTER 17

Victory Celebrations

Glorious celebrations of victory erupted all over the city. Two days later, formal celebrations began with a grand parade through the main thoroughfare to the palace. The grand parade began at the southwest gate and proceeded through the streets to the palace. Girls skipped ahead of the parade, scattering flower petals, and throngs of people lined the streets. Women waved from balconies, laughed, and threw garlands down onto the parade.

General Alexander and his staff marched at the head of the parade. Every man wore his finest armor, polished and buffed to a bright sheen. The general wore a purple cape draped across his back and an elaborate Roman gladius at his side. Behind the general and his staff, two men carried a large, gilded cross. The Templar guard was next, wearing brightly shining armor and red Templar crosses emblazoned on their breastplates.

Next, the sixth legion marched in lockstep. At their head was the ancient staff of the sixth legion, borne by the soldier of honor who had showed the most bravery during the battle. Then came John, carried on a litter and dressed in his finest toga and tunic. Behind him, came his men, walking, laughing, crying, and, when they could, kissing the girls who lined the parade route. After them came the cannons and trebuchets. They were polished and decorated with garlands of flowers. Then the citizen soldiers came, those who had manned the walls, formed the fighting reserve, and operated guns, trebuchets, and catapults.

Reaching the palace, the army was arrayed in formation. In front of the palace there had been built a tall stage, upon which sat Archbishop Gregory and his ministers. Trumpets and drums played martial music. Heroes of the battle were presented before the archbishop, who bestowed honors upon them. At each bestowal of honor, a cheer went up from the crowd. General Alexander announced John's name and asked him to ascend the stage, where he bowed before Archbishop Gregory. A large golden medallion on a royal purple satin ribbon was placed around his neck. When John arose, he faced the crowd and the army. Though he felt joyous about the victory, he still felt deep sadness as he smelled the smoke from funeral pyres, whose fumes rose skyward from land behind the hospital.

CHAPTER 18

Hospital Salvation

With the conclusion of the victory ceremonies, John went past the hospital and noticed bodies being carried out to the open lot behind it. There the bodies were claimed by and released to the families. Any unclaimed body was moved outside the city wall closest to the hospital and cremated there.

John awoke the next morning with a new mission in mind. He sent a messenger to the palace and asked for an audience with Archbishop Gregory. He was determined to improve the lot of the poor patients in hospital and of any men who might be wounded by future wars. Just after noon, he received a reply. The archbishop would see him the following morning.

John spent the rest of the day drawing up plans. The following day, he dressed in his finest attire and arrived at the appointed hour, where he was taken to the throne room. He was used to seeing the archbishop dressed as a Caesar. The other dignitaries and courtiers were in attendance.

"May it please you," John began, "I have observed the poor and wretched circumstances of the sick and injured in our city. I desire, no, I demand that I be allowed to concentrate my time and resources on alleviating their plight. This I will do with as much enthusiasm and success as you have seen with my successful engines of war."

Archbishop Gregory said, "Sir, we have been aware of their plight for a long time. It has been generally assumed that their suffering is the will of God. Do you mean to go against God's will?"

John paused before he spoke. "No . . . no . . . I do not. Is it the will of God, to see his own people suffer and die? Is it not right for someone who has the knowledge to improve the situation . . . or at least try?"

Archbishop Gregory thought for a moment, eyeing John intently. Then he spoke, "If I let you try, you promise me that you will not call on the powers of Satan, and perform miracles!"

He responded, "I promise you sir, that I have no such powers. And I do not desire them. All I ask is that I'd be allowed to try and that you give orders to the hospital authorities not to interfere and to cooperate."

Archbishop Gregory consented to the proposal.

John gathered his workers together and briefed them on his audience with the archbishop. He outlined the plan of attack on death in the hospital and spent the next two days instructing them on hygiene and the care of wounds. He had a little knowledge of this subject because during two summer breaks from college he had worked as an orderly and a nurse's aide. Now he wished he had antibiotics, but none existed.

The next best thing was to try to develop an antiseptic. He knew that wine existed and wondered whether other types of alcohol existed as well. Two of his workers told him that beer could be bought in the market, so John sent them to buy some. Next, he helped the metalworkers fashion a still. John boiled the wine and beer in a large kettle and the evaporated alcohol was collected into a tube and allowed to cool. This allowed the alcohol to concentrate for use an antiseptic.

John and his workers entered the hospital on a day when deaths were increasing. The first task was to get the refuse loaded up and moved outside the city walls, where the refuse was to be burned. The shutters on the hospital windows were opened to allow the movement of air throughout the building. John instructed the nurses and doctors to wash their hands with soap between patients. At first, there was strong resistance to this, but John had only to remind them of Archbishop Gregory's order.

Next, John taught the hospital workers, including the doctors and barbers, about cleansing wounds and using alcohol as an antiseptic. He also taught them that all drinking water was first to be boiled before it was given to patients or staff.

Previously, the barber-surgeons had worn their needle and thread in the lapels of their tunics as a badge of honor. John threatened to report to Archbishop Gregory any such badges of honor. He insisted that the needles and thread be sterilized in boiling water or alcohol before use. Likewise, he insisted that all instruments and utensils be boiled in water or soaked in alcohol.

Over the course of several months, a remarkable thing happened: the death rate dropped by two-thirds. Going to the hospital was no longer a death sentence. The mood in the institution changed to hopefulness. There were still holdouts among the medical staff, who thought it was beneath them to wash their hands. But they couldn't deny the results. Still, some became envious of John's success.

One day, John brought his new microscope to the hospital and announced that he was going to hold a seminar on germ theory. During the seminar, he brought out the microscope, placed some water from a stagnant pool on the microscope's stage, and adjusted the scope. He allowed anyone who was interested to view the wonders of the microscopic world—that is, the dirt and small "animals" in the stagnant water. By doing this John hoped the demonstration would convince the hospital workers why the water had to be boiled.

CHAPTER 19

An Evening at Home with Friends

During these months of working at the hospital, John's love for Catherine grew. He invited her to have dinner with him as often as possible, at her house, his house, or a café. They spent long hours walking in the evening, talking and dreaming. Catherine wanted to marry and be the wife of a prominent man within the community. Her desire for children and the finer things in life was obvious. John talked instead of ideas and projects that he envisioned for the future and of the great advances possible because of the technology that he could develop, based on his rudimentary understanding of science.

One night John decided to have a dinner party. He and his servants worked for two days making preparations for it. On the night of the gathering, his guests started arriving early. Catherine and her family were there to help as co hosts. The foundry man and his helpers were the first to arrive. Some of John's own employees were guests of honor. The commissioners of housing, finance, medical care, education, and others were invited. Some came, but some did not. General Alexander was invited but could not attend, and he sent his executive officer to represent him. Ordinary soldiers that John had met were invited as well as ordinary citizens. The deputy chief of staff of the hospital was also in attendance. All counted, about three dozen guests arrived for the festivities. The gathering was truly democratic and included people from the most humble citizens to some of the most powerful.

The meal was held in the great dining hall of his residence. The hall was large and featured brightly painted frescos showing saints and martyrs. Niches with beautiful statuary adorned the walls. The floor showed a mosaic depicting the Virgin Mary and the Christ child surrounded by angels and shepherds. To one side of the dining hall in an apse was a small shrine with a cross and portraits of John's previous wife and children painted on the sides of the altar. A large oak table was in the center of the room, and a wide fireplace in one wall provided heat. Wine, roasted lamb and boar were featured. Figs, dates, and olives were in abundance. Several types of bread served with butter and jam were strategically placed in front of every four to six guests. Pears and apples alternated at each place setting on the long table. Bunches of freshly picked grapes provided an appetizer. Beans and other legumes were served with the main course. The main course was prepared in an open pit and had been cooked all day. Other enticing vegetables that John was not familiar with were prepared by his servants and served as side dishes.

John said grace, but perhaps not with the same conviction. "Our Lord and Father, bless this bounty of yours which we are about to receive. This we do in the name of your son Jesus Christ and the Holy Ghost. Amen."

Conversation began with a discussion of the war and each participant's role in it. That discussion evolved into a deeper conversation about the work being done at the hospital. Each person was curious about how John could have accomplished such a dramatic drop in the death rate.

He said, "It is nothing more than basic science. The largest killer of patients is infection."

A murmur arose from the guests. "Infection?"

"Yes," said John. "Infection is the growth of very small animals or germs in the wounds, lungs, and other tissues and organs of the patients."

One of the commissioners replied, "Come on, you would have us believe in some small creatures we cannot even see that cause the suffering and death of those poor, wretched souls!"

John retorted, "Sir, you cannot see God, yet you believe in him. And with the changes that have been made to fight such unseen animalcules, the result is a drop in the death rate and more patients alive to go home to their families."

The executive officer of the army entered the conversation. "Sir, the change of the death rate is a miracle of God, for only God has the power to save lives. His will be done."

Again, John replied, "No, sir, it is not God, and it is science. And given enough time, we could develop medicines to fight even more infections and diseases. Surely these results could not have been accomplished without the will of God. Why not use these gifts to benefit all of mankind?"

The executive officer replied, "To benefit the infidels, too?"

John didn't reply to that last question. The deputy chief of staff of the hospital kept quiet.

Changing the subject, John said, "General, what do you think of the telescope?"

The general responded, "A very good invention. Now we can know what the enemy is doing before he himself does."

All in attendance cried, "Yes, yes, bravo!"

"Thank you," John said.

The commissioner of education asked, "How did you ever design the telescope?"

"Optics or the science of optics, to be more exact," John said. "Light travels in straight lines, but in transparent material like glass, if the shape of the glass is right, the light will bend. That bending of light can enlarge objects at a distance, very small or very far away. I wish I had studied that more in school."

The commissioner of education interrupted him. "In school? We don't teach that! Why, we have never heard of that before."

"No, sorry. I meant to say my school," John replied. "There are formulas and principles that apply to all light and therefore to optics. That is the science of grinding lens to specific shapes so as to refocus light and make it do what you want. Would you like to see my latest telescope? It is much more powerful than the previous ones."

As the meal was nearly finished, most of the guests went up onto the roof of John's house to see the new telescope. It was three times the size of the ones used in the war. It was made somewhat like a barrel, with wood staves forming a cylinder with iron hoops or rings holding them in place. The lenses were mounted inside the wood cylinder. It was mounted on a wood stand that could easily be swiveled to be pointed to any direction of the compass. The telescope could with a light touch be pointed at any elevation above the horizon. Others excused themselves and, John hoped, went home to think.

The night was pleasant and clear. The stars were shining brightly and could be easily identified. John could trace the path that the planets followed from east to west. His new telescope was much larger than the first one, and he could adjust the focus by pushing the eyepiece lens in and out of the telescope tube. First, he pointed out the constellations that he could remember. Most people there knew of them. Then he pointed the telescope at Jupiter, focused carefully, and invited his guests to look through the telescope at the distant planet.

His guests were astonished. As plain as day, they could see the multicolored disk of the planet and four of its moons. John explained that Jupiter is a planet or what the ancients called wandering stars. "Jupiter is the largest planet in the solar system," he said. "It has a system of moons, some of which could possibly harbor life. And if it has moons going around it, then the earth can go around the sun. Jupiter is a large ball of gas."

One of the observers exclaimed, "A ball of gas? Then why doesn't Jupiter float off and disappear?"

John chuckled and said, "Gravity, the force that holds us here on earth, holds the planets together, even gaseous ones. It is thought that there are eight planets."

Again someone interrupted and said, "We were taught there are only five, not including the earth."

John replied, "No, there are eight that we know of. The other planets are so very far away that they cannot be seen with your eyes. They can be seen with telescopes, but not mine. It isn't strong enough." When they had all had a chance to see Jupiter, John next aimed the telescope at Mars. They could see the red disk of that planet, with a hint of a polar ice cap.

"Mars is most like our earth. It has clouds and air; however, you could not live by breathing its air. Mars is slightly smaller than the earth and has two moons. You could jump three times the height on Mars that you can jump here. It has a reddish hue because its ground is red, and most of that color is due to the rust in the soil. Mars may at one time have had running water and life. It is a dead world now."

"Its inhabitants must have made God mad, and he destroyed them," one man said. Everyone stopped peering through the telescope and turned to John.

John said, "No, Mars never did have intelligent life that we know of."

The last planet, they viewed was Saturn, which was magnificent. The telescope showed the planet's rings and several of its moons. John explained, "Saturn is the second largest planet in the solar system, and scientists know that its density is such that it would float on water."

"Den-sity," someone remarked. "What is that?"

"Density is the weight of something per volume," John said. "For example, the weight of a piece of gold is greater than a piece of wood of the same size, right?"

Everyone agreed that John's statement was correct. Then one of the women asked, "What are the rings of Saturn made of?"

John said, "We don't know for sure, but they appear to be mainly ice and rock. Some of the ring components are as small as grains of sand, and some are as big as houses. I have been told that they may be the remains of a moon that was torn apart by the gravity of the planet."

"A world destroyed by God," remarked one of the guests.

The telescope inquiries lasted until early morning. All of John's guests were much impressed, and finally they left, having asked more questions than John could answer. He thought the night and the dinner party had been very successful.

CHAPTER 20

The Heretic

Several days later, while John was working at the hospital, a squad of soldiers appeared. They asked for John and were escorted to him by one physician and several hospital workers. At the time, John was showing another physician how to use the microscope to count blood cells and how that information could be beneficial to the patients.

The captain of the guard asked, "Are you Master John Pope?"

"Yes, I am. What is the meaning of this intrusion into my work?"

The response was swift and matter-of-fact. "Sir, you are being arrested for heresy and blasphemy. You must accompany us, or we will take you by force."

John staggered in disbelief and dread. "I will accompany you, sir. Where are we going?"

"To the palace, sir."

Seeing a little bit of hope, John said, "Then I can talk to Archbishop Gregory about this misunderstanding."

"No, sir, my orders are to take you to the dungeon until trial. It was the archbishop who gave the order."

Stunned and shaking, John walked between two ranks of soldiers in the cold drizzle. On the slow, agonizing march, he noticed that common people and others he knew were pointing at him and whispering.

He was led down the stairs to the dungeon and into a room filled with jail cells. John was familiar with this place from his experience with Timothy. The heavy door creaked opened, and the brawny guards threw John across the dungeon floor, slamming him into the wall on the other side. Before he could turn around, the door was shut, and he heard the lock being turned.

The cell was dark and dank and smelled of feces and urine. It took awhile for John's eyes to adjust to the dim light. A pallet of straw and a honey pot rested on the cold, stone floor next to the wall. Then he noticed another figure leaning up against the wall. The man had long, dark brown hair, a full beard, and olive-toned skin. His tunic was of coarsely woven wool, and he wore rough, leather sandals. He had bruises and cuts about his head and neck and marks on his forearms where, John guessed, he had raised his arms to protect his head from blows. Their eyes met, and the man smiled.

"Are you hurt? Did they torture you?" asked the man.

"No, I'm not hurt, and I haven't been tortured. But I don't know why I'm here."

The man seemed very gentle. He came over to John, put his arm around him, and helped him to sit down.

"What happened?" he asked John"

John felt somehow secure in the man's presence and began relating the story. He did not tell him the whole story, but only the part following the massacre of his family to the present.

"Now," John concluded, "I've been accused of heresy and blasphemy. I don't know what my accusers mean or what evidence they have."

"I know it's hard to understand," the stranger said. "I, too, have been accused of heresy and blasphemy."

John was surprised. This man seemed so gentle. "For what?" John asked.

"Love," the gentle stranger responded.

"For love? How is that heresy or blasphemy?"

"I come from a village on the shore of the large, freshwater lake," the stranger said. "We are simple fishermen and farmers who care only about feeding our families and treating each person with compassion, respect, and justice. Our village has been conquered and re-conquered many times over the past centuries, first by one group and then another group. Each had an idea or vision of who or what God is and how he should be worshiped and respected. If you did not do it their way, you would be cast out and damned to hell if you were lucky. The unlucky ones—and those were the majority—were executed in the name of God."

The stranger smiled. "Each group claimed to have the truth, but it became increasingly difficult to determine what the truth is. Gradually I understood that they had all lost what it meant to respect and love God."

John found himself fascinated by the gentle stranger, whose story was at least as compelling as his own. He sank down onto the floor, oblivious to its filth, and listened as the stranger continued.

"The idea came to me that God is not so much a who as a what. He means loving your neighbor with compassion, justice, and respect, no matter who that neighbor may be. God means equality among all people, no matter their race, nationality, creed, or gender. What God means is enlightenment. This was the message we spread—that is, my colleagues and I. Of course, our work eventually reached the authorities here. I came here to spread the message to the city, after spending several years spreading it elsewhere. And here they arrested me for doing this work."

"Did you get a trial?"

"Yes, a trial of sorts."

"What do you mean of sorts?" John asked.

"It was a trial, but a religious trial with the outcome preordained."

"This makes me wonder about my trial and fate. Did they give you a chance to defend yourself?"

"They did, but your fate is in the hands of God, my son."

John frowned. "They speak of the Scriptures as the ultimate law, the word of God himself, the ultimate truth. Are the Scriptures really all that?"

The heretic replied, "The holy books were not written by God, but by man in his feeble attempt to understand and mold the Almighty to his own ideas of who and what God is. These differences in understandings have led to conflicts. And remember that, in their eyes, what I speak is heresy and blasphemy."

John, "I just don't understand what I've done. How can bringing information about the world, about how to help their sick, about how inventing machines can defend their city . . . how can that knowledge be dangerous?"

The heretic smiled again. "My son, what you bring is knowledge that is threatening to their limited view of the universe. What you have said violates their belief and understanding. And that challenge seems dangerous to them. All people, indeed, were made in God's image, but not necessarily his physical image. We share God's ability to think, reason, question, investigate, and create. Knowledge is God's gift to us. Most knowledge is neutral, some is beneficial, and some is not. The nature of knowledge depends on our use of it."

Sitting down on the floor beside John, the stranger continued in a soothing voice. "You showed them that Earth and, by extension, they themselves are not the center of the universe or the reason for existence. That information is both humbling and threatening. You also showed them that by understanding how nature works, they gain a form of self-knowledge. Again, that kind of knowledge can be threatening."

"Everything changes," John said. "Is that truth so frightening?"

"It can be frightening," the stranger said. "You have exposed to them that nature and our knowledge are always changing. They do not like change because they cannot predict it, and thus they feel less secure. If knowledge changes, then maybe their interpretations of the Scriptures must change. And that is threatening."

John listened raptly as the heretic continued. "By trying to stifle change, they encourage it, but in a more sinister direction, as you have seen. The only way to judge and adapt to those changes is with the help of that part of God that is love, respect, compassion, and knowledge—or enlightenment. "

John asked, "And who is or what is God?" He was transfixed by this gentle, wise, apparently common man.

"God is a concept," the heretic said, "for that is only how we can know him or understand him in our limited human way. We refer to him in human terms such as Lord and Father. And, in way, God is a parent, but not in the usual human understanding. We were created by him, but not in the sense of being molded from soil— for that is only a metaphor. We are children of the cosmos. And God is the cosmos and more."

"Tell me, please," John said, "what about the Bible stories of Genesis, Noah, David, Solomon, Moses, and Jesus, or even Mohammed and the Koran?"

The heretic replied, "Many of the personages in the holy texts did exist, but a mythology grew up around them that is far grander and more mystical than they actually were. Some of the stories have their basis in actual historical events, but the facts are less important than the stories. Remember, the stories' value lies in what they teach and in their attempt to help men understand God from a human viewpoint. "

"Is this true for other holy books?" John asked.

The gentle stranger said, "Usually, yes."

An epiphany was coming to John. But before he could ask more questions, the cell door opened, and two guards entered to escort John to trial.

CHAPTER 21

Trial

The courtroom in the palace had an impressive appearance with its marble walls and floor. Statues of saints and heroes of the Bible decorated niches in the walls. A mosaic of the Ten Commandments was prominently displayed above the tribunal judges' bench. There was no jury box. A dock was prominently placed before the bench, and a gallery stood behind the dock. Off to the side was a witness stand.

Two armed guards escorted John to the dock. The galleries filled quickly and prominent among the attendees were Catherine, her father, and his shop workers. The judges, two bishops and the archbishop, entered, dressed in their finest robes. The archbishop, who presided, rapped his gavel to call the court to order. A priest uttered a short prayer, and the archbishop gave permission for all to be seated, except John.

Two priests were to act as prosecutors. John had no defense attorney, so he would have to defend himself. The only evidence he could offer was his word and the observations of witnesses.

The archbishop asked the sergeant at arms of the court to read the indictment.

He began, "May it please the court that on numerous occasions, the defendant, John Pope, did willfully speak of and try to induce others to question facts and policies of the Holy Church. The charge is heresy and blasphemy."

The lead prosecutor said, "We will show by affidavit, witness, and evidence that the accused, although a hero of the late war, did knowingly and willfully subvert the church and its teachings. For we all must be on guard against the schemes of the devil."

The second prosecutor said, "The accused, at a social gathering in his home, demonstrated an instrument of Satan. With this instrument and trickery, he had his guests believe that they were seeing another world, indeed, several worlds. I call the commissioner of merchants to the stand."

The commissioner rose and strode to the witness stand, dressed in a scarlet tunic and toga. He took the stand and swore to Almighty God, with one hand on the Bible, to tell the whole truth.

The prosecutor asked him, "Do you know the accused?"

"Yes, I do."

"How and in what capacity do you know him?"

"He is an eager and talented young man," the commissioner said. "He came to me with an idea to protect the city and the faith. He also thought that he could turn it into a business and make a living. He presented the idea very well, and I became very enthusiastic." In a hesitant, hushed voice, he added, "He is also my daughter's fiancé."

"Were you at his house the night in question?" the prosecutor asked.

"I was."

"And what did you see and hear?"

"He showed us a new version of his telescope. It was similar to the one used in the war. But it was much stronger. He took us up on the roof of his house and showed us certain stars, the type known to our astrologers as wandering stars. These stars pass through the zodiac and thereby can be used to foresee events along with other uses that I am not familiar with. These planets, as John called them, circle the sun, not the earth. Some of these worlds have their own worlds circling them."

The prosecutor dismissed the commissioner. Several more witnesses were called and related the same story. John was not allowed to cross-examine the witnesses.

The prosecutor produced the telescope and invited the tribunal to examine it. The tribunal members did so and seemed to find the instrument amusing.

The prosecutor said, "This device tricks you into thinking and believing that the earth and the planets revolve around the sun. Do we not know from our great thinkers of the past that the heavens exist on crystal spheres and revolve around the earth? And if these crystals do not exist around the earth, and if the earth is not the center of the universe, then where are heaven and God?"

John wanted to interrupt, but he dared not do so. He could only listen helpless as the prosecutor continued. "If these planets are circling the sun in the firmament—or what the accused told one of the witnesses is called 'space'—what keeps the planets from falling into the sun? For that matter, what keeps us from falling into the sun? Or what keeps us from flying off into oblivion? It is God."

At last John was allowed to respond. He empathized with what Galileo must have gone through when he was tried and found guilty of heresy in 1633. But John had to try, at least.

"The telescope shows that there are many more worlds than ours alone," John began. "And each world can have its own system of small moons or worlds orbiting it. And maybe there could be life on some of those worlds."

The people in the gallery cried, "Blasphemy!"

But John continued. "Why is that information so threatening to you? What is so blasphemous about that statement? What it does reveal is that the world or the universe is much larger and grander than what any one of us think. What keeps the planets circling the sun is a force called gravity, or the attraction between two bodies with masses."

He took a deep breath, looked around the room and found Catherine in the gallery. He then moved in front of the gallery. "We do not fly off the earth because we are kept here by gravity. The planets do not fall into the sun because of the speed of the planets equal the force of gravity. It is a law of nature. Maybe some of the old teachings are wrong. May it please the court to let me prove the powers of the telescope? Tonight, if the stars are bright, I would like to set up the telescope outside in the plaza of the palace and show you the wonders."

"I object!" bellowed the lead prosecutor.

"On what grounds?" asked one of the bishops.

"On the grounds that this instrument is a device of the devil. And it should not be used to corrupt the court!" the lead prosecutor retorted.

"Objection sustained," Archbishop Gregory said.

"But why?" John said. "If I cannot introduce evidence, then how can I prove my case?"

A bishop replied, "Evidence is in the Bible, not in the telescope. We will decide which evidence is allowable and true."

The lead prosecutor stood. "Here is another invention that the accused produced to deceive our healers. This is what the accused calls a microscope." He passed that instrument to the tribunal to examine and then called his first witness, the chief physician at the hospital. After the swearing-in, he asked the distinguished physician, "Doctor, are you familiar with Mr. John Pope? Also, are you familiar with this device?"

Chief physician responded, "Yes, I am familiar with both. John showed the microscope to us after the death rate started dropping in the hospital. He showed us what he called germs that live in raw water. He said these animalcules cause the fevers and pus in the patients. He said they were responsible for pneumonia and other types of what he called infections. He said these animalcules can be killed by boiling the water and treating wounds with the alcohol antiseptic. He said we had to burn all discarded dressings and refuse to kill the breeding grounds of these germs. I have never heard of such a thing. Life and death is the province of God, not man or unseen animalcules. Yet, with the measures John instituted, the number of deaths did decline."

"What more can you add?" asked the prosecutor.

"Well, I overheard him mumble many times that if only he could get drugs from his world, he could save many more lives," said the physician. "I did not know what he meant by 'his world.' Was he the devil, and is his world hell? He did on one occasion show us some blood under his microscope. The blood contained what he called cells. Indeed, he said our whole bodies are made up of billions of cells. He said that when these cells get sick, they cause disease."

Several more witnesses from the hospital were called, and all related similar stories.

Rising in his own defense, John spoke. "The death rate in the hospital was totally unacceptable. To be admitted to the hospital was essentially a death sentence. The largest percentage of those deaths was the fault of ignorance and poor hygiene, not the will of God. Infection is by far the largest killer in this world." John paused for moment looked around the court room studying the expressions on the faces of those present. Then he continued, "Infection is due to germs. These germs or animalcules require a microscope to be seen. They are far smaller than what we can detect with our own eyes. The microscope helps us extend our vision, the same way the telescope extends our vision in the opposite direction. Germs require stagnant water or other environments to grow and reproduce. Once they gain access to our body, they continue growing and reproducing. The fevers and pus are the manifestations of these life forms living within the human body. So if we can eliminate the environments the organisms need to live on and in, we can decrease the amount of disease they produce. By properly disposing of waste and soiled dressings, we have been able to decrease the death rate at the hospital. By using a chemical, such as alcohol, to sterilize instruments and to clean and sterilize the sutures used to close wounds, we can decrease the death rate even more." Taking a breath and collecting his thoughts he continued, "There are certain drugs, or there could be, that could be given to patients by mouth or placed directly into their bloodstream that would kill these germs without hurting the patients. There are even some germs too small for the microscope to see, and those tiny germs also cause illness and death. An example of this is the disease that you call the pox. Our bodies made of billions of small cells. And if they get sick, that manifests as disease. An example here is cancer, known as tumor. It is the manifestation of cells growing wildly out of control. The blood has two kinds of cells, white and red. The white blood cells fight infection and the red carry oxygen to the body and carry away waste."

At that point, one bishop sitting beside the Archbishop asked, "What is oxygen?"

John responded, "Oxygen is a component of the air that allows us to live. If we don't have oxygen, we die. Fire will not burn without oxygen."

The other bishop said, "Would you have us believe that disease and suffering are caused by animals so small that we can't even see them? Further, would you have us believe that the air has some kind of substance in it that we cannot see, but that allows a fire to burn and for life to exist? I find this preposterous. It is fanciful. It must be the workings of Satan. This is blasphemy. Let's have the next witness!"

John begged, "May I at least show you how the microscope works? We can do it here and now."

To which Archbishop Gregory responded confidently, "No."

John shouted, "You don't even allow me the right or courtesy of a demonstration to defend my words. What you are doing is hypocrisy. It is an outrage! It is . . ."

"Gag the prisoner! And restrain him!" roared the archbishop. "No disrespect will come from the prisoner as to this honorable court." The sergeant at arms and two Templar knights immediately restrained John and gagged him. The members of the tribunal whispered to one another and then looked at John.

The archbishop said, "If you behave, I will have the bonds and gag removed. Do you promise?"

John nodded in the affirmative. The gag and bonds were removed. John felt terrible fear running through his body.

The second prosecutor called Catherine to the stand. She was sworn in.

"My lady, what is your relationship with the accused?" the prosecutor began.

"I am his betrothed," said Catherine meekly.

"What do you know of his business and actions?"

She responded, "Not much. He would talk of plans, inventions, and discoveries that could change this world. He is a good man, and he has saved the city! I love him."

"I'm sure you do. What are these plans and discoveries?"

Very quietly, Catherine said, "He talked of the knowledge that he'd had before. It was based on science and technology derived from science. He said that not only could we increase food production with it, but we could improve the plight of the sick and the poor, speed up transportation, and accomplish many other things."

"What did he mean by 'before'?"

Catherine's tears began running down her cheeks, and her voice and hands began to tremble. "I don't know. He talked of another world he once was a part of. He talked of many wondrous things—machines that could fly and even go to the moon, and carts or chariots that could move without horses to travel between cities."

The prosecutor turned to the tribunal and said, "Flying, going to the moon, and horseless chariots. This is all witchcraft." Turning to face Catherine, he asked, "And what is his impression of our world?"

John interrupted, "No, Catherine, no. Those are ideas that you only ask in your heart and confide in with those closest!"

"Enough! Silence! Let the witness speak, or you will be restrained and gagged!" cried the archbishop.

John looked even more afraid, still shaking his head no at Catherine and trying to tell her not to say any more.

Catherine paused, dried her tears, and looked at John and then at her father in apprehension and resignation. With her lips trembling, she said, "He said that this world is retarded in its development. No one is free to question authority. This world practices mind control. No one is allowed to be curious or inquisitive without the permission of the church. The result is a perpetual dark age. Each religion, citing its own dogma and claiming final truth, detests competition from other religions. Because none of the religions are willing to compromise, then. . . ."

John shouted, "No, Catherine, no!" He was afraid for her. The guards grabbed him, but their attention was on Catherine.

She put her face in her hands and wept. She knew that she had been forced to betray him. All was quiet in the courtroom. John stood there, helpless. The guards released their hold on him as he began to weep quietly.

The archbishop spoke, "The witness is excused." Catherine's father led her out of the courtroom.

The archbishop announced, "This court is in recess until tomorrow, at which time testimony will continue, and the defendant will be allowed to state his defense."

John was taken again to the palace dungeon.

He was angry and asked the heretic, "Why I am not allowed to defend myself with evidence?

"Because evidence can show their arguments to be hollow, without substance. To be able to prove what you are saying is to disprove their authority. Authority cannot allow itself to be shown empty. You noticed that the archbishop is the presiding judge. The city and most states here, whether they are Christian, Hebrew, Muslim, or any other, are theocracies—that is, they are rule by means of religion. The ruler claims to have the ear and voice of God. Therefore he rules in the name of God for God. Do you really think God wants to rule his people? Do you think God would want to communicate only to these men?"

"No, I don't."

"The rulers rule by their own hand, not God's," the heretic said. "With the propaganda of God's rule. They trick the people into thinking their rule is legal. The archbishop presides as chief judge to do two things—first, to uphold the illusion of legitimate rule under God, and second, to make sure what is decided benefits the state. And they are state."

John felt depressed. "The trial is rigged. I have no chance."

"No, not necessarily. Remember there are two other judges, and if you make strong argument in your defense, it is not unreasonable for them to grant clemency. It's going to be difficult. It isn't over yet."

John and the heretic ate the porridge and stale bread provided for the evening's meal. Neither talked much that night after dinner; instead, they kept their own thoughts company. John went over the day's events in his mind, trying to come up with a strategy for his defense.

Early the next morning, the guards appeared and took John by the arms into the courtroom and placed him in the dock.

The two bishops and the archbishop entered the court and took their places at the bench, and the archbishop gave permission for all to be seated, except John. The gallery was crowded, and the courtroom was hot with summer heat. Archbishop Gregory called the sergeant at arms of the court over to the bench and whispered in his ear. The sergeant went over to the windows and opened them for a breath of air.

Rising from his chair at the table, the prosecutor strode over to the dock to face John.

"Sir, could you please explain the magic powder that you invented?"

Taking a large breath and glancing at Catherine, John began. "Gunpowder is not magic. It is made by basic chemistry and follows fundamental laws of nature. It requires three ingredients: charcoal, sulfur—or what you call brimstone—and saltpeter. Mixing them carefully in the proper proportions can produce a black powder that can burn quickly. The gases given off by that burning can produce enough pressure to create an explosion or hurl a projectile. Everything all substances are made of molecules, and molecules are made of atoms. Atoms are the basic building blocks of matter."

"Are not the four basic constituents of matter are fire, water, earth, and air?" asked the prosecutor.

"No," said John. "Water, earth, and air are themselves made up of atoms, which make up molecules. Fire is energy being released by a chemical reaction. This energy release we see and feel as light and heat. What is left after the chemical reaction and release of energy is another type of compound or a new arrangement of atoms in molecules."

The prosecutor said, "Alchemists have been attempting to turn base metals into gold for centuries. With this knowledge, could you do what they cannot?"

"No," John said. "I can't change base metal to gold. That takes another type of reaction to convert one type of atom into another. That is not black magic, but it is science."

The prosecutor faced the tribunal and said, "Only God has the power to create or destroy or change matter. The accused claims that power, also. Where did he learn this power? Who taught him this knowledge— God or Satan? This is divine wisdom that is not given to mortal man."

Turning back to face John, the prosecutor asked, "Do you believe that God created man?"

John thought for a while before answering and said, "I did at one time, but now I don't know, at least in the sense you mean. I now think the scientists of my world are right. I now understand that science has to work from observation and experiment, without consideration of the divine, if it is to make any progress at all. And from that perspective, man did evolve from lower forms of life— specifically, apes. The lines of evidence for evolution come from many sources. They also show that all men are related. We are all one species, one people."

Ignoring the shocked remarks and comments from the gallery, John said, "I'm now beginning to see the sacred in that concept. Indeed, we are all connected with all other forms of life on this planet. It was silly, arrogant, and stupid of me to ignore the evidence or deny it, as you are doing now. According to my world's science, man evolved from apes a few million years ago."

The prosecutor sounded as amazed as anyone in the gallery. "You do not believe that we are divine creations of God? Do you not know that creation began in 4004 BC? Would you have us believe that we came from apes? That idea is preposterous!"

John allowed himself a smile. "We are divine creations in a sense, and I would like to think that God did have a hand in our evolution, but not as traditionally thought. Maybe we are not meant to know how God influenced creation. As for the idea that creation began in 4004 B.C., I know that the calculation was based on the lives of Biblical figures by a Bishop James Ussher whose work was first published in 1650, but was not based on any type of scientific evidence."

As the courtroom continued to buzz with astonishment, John said, "That creation story has some truth, but not literal truth. It is a metaphor. The earth is actually far older than the date given by Bishop Ussher. According to scientists from my world, the earth is more than four billion years old. Anyway, what is wrong with being descended from apes? I used to think that concept was terrible, but now I don't. Indeed, it has majesty of its own. What is wrong with being related to all other life on earth? I see a far grander and mystical sense in that concept than saying that we were created de novo in God's image. And what does the phrase in the Bible that says 'created in his image' actually mean? Does that mean we really look like God, or does it mean we have the same attributes of consciousness, thinking, reasoning, and creativity? If God indeed looks like us, then he is limited and, therefore, could not be omniscient. If there is a God, then our concept of who or what he is has to change, to evolve. Are we divine creations? No, not in a supernatural sense. But I see the sacred in the curiosity of a child asking why, how, and when. I see the divine in our appreciation of beauty, our growing comprehension of nature, and our compassion for others. If this be heresy, then I am a heretic. But if you see the truth in what I say, then how can this be heresy, and how can I be blaspheming God?"

All was quiet in the courtroom. They all seemed to know that John convicted himself.

After a few moments, the lead prosecutor said, "There you have it, revered judges. The accused has convicted himself. You heard him! He talks of his world, the world of science, the world of demons and witchcraft. He scoffs at the facts of the Bible. We do not have to prove anything because it is the word of God. And where is his proof?"

Archbishop Gregory said, "We shall recess until tomorrow to deliberate our verdict." Then John was escorted back to his cell under armed guard.

CHAPTER 22

Trial Outcome

In the cell again, John faced the other heretic, who asked, ""All did not go well?""

John replied, "No, I convicted myself. I talked too much. But I see and understand now that blind faith in a religion can itself become evil— even if, in the beginning, religion didn't start out as evil. I can see how religion can suppress and control the acquisition of knowledge to keep itself in power'. Faith or religion itself must evolve to stay relevant. If it does not, then it will change in an awful way. If there is a God, I cannot believe that he would not want us to discover and learn the laws of nature. By discovering those laws, we not only progress technically, we also come closer to understanding ourselves and God. And God does not want to rule us. He wants to love us as a parent does."

"Every chip in their wall of superstition and unreasonable faith is the beginning of a crack that will eventually lead to the collapse of the wall," the heretic said. "There are many walls around many superstitions and faiths; they all must be brought down if there is ever to be a true appreciation of who and what God is and what man's true place is in creation. We are not heretics; we are prophets, and in some cases, we must become martyrs, for this view". Now tell me about yourself. Who are your parents? Do you have any brothers and sisters?"

John sat back, half closing his eyes, and a subtle smile appeared on his lips. "My father built houses and buildings. He died when I was in college. I miss him very much, but I blame him for becoming a pastor originally and delivering lay sermons. My mother grew up during a great time of stress in our country. She encouraged me to learn and to be self-sufficient. I have a brother and a sister. We were never very close. I miss them now more than I ever have. You know I was married and had two wonderful children. My wife and children are dead now, killed by religious fanatics of Islam." Tears started running down his cheeks.

The heretic held his hand, smiled, and offered a little consolation. "Fanatics of any religion commit atrocities in the name of God. They believe that God tells them to do such things. That is untrue. The fanatics do them because that is what their own warped minds are telling them to do. God fears religious fanatics more than any other. Their impulses lead to far more destructive and ruthless war than any other and their actions lead people away from God."

A cold realization came over John.

The gentle man continued, "You have had great people in your life. They may be dead, but they are still a part of you. Therefore, they still live. Cherish the times you had with them. No one dies in vain if he is loved."

"I became very angry at my best friend the last time I saw him," John said tearfully. "I walked out on him, cursing him."

"He knows that you didn't mean it," the stranger said. "He will still be your friend. When you get a chance, you need to contact him and apologize. Then you can work out your differences. True friendship is tested by such emotions as anger, but it is never destroyed."

"What about you?" John asked. "Where are your parents and brothers and sisters?"

The man replied with a smile, "My father was a carpenter. Like your father, he built things. My mother is still alive, but I don't know where she is now. I have many brothers and sisters. Most are married and have lives of their own. My oldest brother works with me and helps in the teachings. He is here in the city, but he hasn't been caught, or at least I hope he hasn't. "

"Are you married?" John asked.

"I have no wife or children. One of my comrades, a woman, is one of the closest friends I have, but I was never meant to be married. That is one of life's pleasures that I fear I will not experience."

They became quiet, and John grew lost in his thoughts. He felt that he was beginning to grasp a wisp of an idea about how he and the stranger could escape, and he described his idea to the heretic.

The man said, ""You may get to the wall and possibly a little way outside it. But you will be caught and brought back. I understand that you must try, and I pray that you will make it. However, I hope that your spirit will not be broken when you are caught and brought back to face your sentence. I will not go with you. I hope you understand.""

John nodded. He did decide to attempt to escape after the verdict was pronounced on the following day. After all, he thought with a glimmer of hope, the verdict could be not guilty.

The next morning, a knock came at the heavy wooden door of the cell. John could hear the keys in the lock.

The captain of the guards stepped in, saying, "Master John Pope, it is time to face the decision."

John was shackled, taken under heavy guard to the courtroom, and was placed in the dock. The gallery was already full.

The sergeant at arms of the court proclaimed, "All rise for the most holy tribunal."

The two bishops and the archbishop entered and took their respective chairs at the bench.

The Archbishop spoke first. "Master John Pope, after much deliberation, we the tribunal find you guilty of heresy and blasphemy. Do you have anything to say before we pronounce the sentence?"

John said, "If I am guilty of a crime against God, then let God do the punishment."

The archbishop replied, "We appreciate your aid in the last war, and we hope that those inventions of yours will continue to be developed. However, that progress does not excuse your guilt. We are instruments of God, and we do his bidding. We must protect the faith, and, therefore we pronounce sentence in the name of God. We hereby order that you be burned at the stake at dawn on the third day."

With that pronouncement, both cheers and gasps arose from the gallery. Catherine let out a loud cry and was led, weeping, from the courtroom by her father. John's legs went limp, and he had to be held up by the guards. Astonishment, disbelief, and fear appeared on his face as his mouth gaped open, and tears began streaming down his cheeks. After he gained some semblance of composure, he was escorted under heavy guard back to his cell.

CHAPTER 23

Escape

I will escape, John thought, and began planning the event down to
the minutest detail. He waited until the evening meal was brought
in. It consisted of porridge and wormy bread. As the door was
swung open and the guard entered, John grabbed him from behind
placing his arm around his neck with the crook of his elbow over the
midline of his neck and with the help of his free hand pinching his
arm together. This is a sleeper hold that would quickly disable an
opponent by pinching the neck arteries and veins thereby cutting off
blood supply to the brain. When the guard was unconscious, John
quickly changed clothes with the guard and started out of the cell.

He stopped and glanced back at the heretic, motioning and
mouthing, "Coming with me?"

The heretic smiled and shook his head no.

John left the cell door slightly ajar, in case the gentle stranger
wanted to follow him later. John made his way through the dungeon
without difficulty, as there were no personnel present, as there were
no tortures being done at that time in the day. Reaching the top of the
stairs, he carefully opened the door and surveyed the scene. There
were no guards anywhere. He soon spotted a soldier with a satchel
walking down the corridor. John then straightened up, opened the
door and motioned for the soldier to come with him down to the
dungeon. As the soldier started down the stairs he again applied the
sleeper hold and disabled him. He took the leather satchel. Then he

started walking down the hall after closing the door to the stairway to the dungeon. When he met someone walking his direction, he would either detour down another hall or look as though he didn't notice the person, as he was too busy looking at the papers he kept in the leather satchel.

He did not want to go out the front door as he was afraid that the guards there would recognize him. He also stayed well away from the vicinity of the throne room. He finally made his way to a wing of the palace and a side exit door. As he was leaving, he heard commotion deep in the palace. Someone must have discovered his escape. The side door in front of him emptied onto an alleyway. He spied some peasant tunics hanging on a clothesline between buildings on either side of the alleyway. He climbed a lattice to a small balcony next to the clothesline and retrieved one of the tunics. Quickly changing into it, he hid the uniform and satchel behind some amphora on the balcony. He then climbed back down the lattice and made his way up the alley.

He didn't want others to have a look at him, as his face was probably familiar to everyone. He thought about making his way to the tunnel that let out underneath the east wall. Then he remembered that the tunnel had been blown up. He couldn't leave by the southwest gate as it was still being reconstructed and strengthened. The west gate would have to be his way out. And to get to it, he would have to pass the hospital.

Walking as quickly as he dared toward the hospital, he passed through a small bazaar. There he stole a leather bag and stocked it with some food and a flask of wine. These supplies were enough for a few days and were enough to get him started toward freedom.

As he passed the hospital, he noticed that the windows were once again shuttered. Refuse and soiled dressings were being dumped in the empty lot. Hadn't the people learned anything from him? Didn't they learn that unless they continued the hygiene and antiseptic procedures, the hospital was going to be again a death house? Old habits are hard to change, he thought.

He continued on his way to the west gate. Hiding in doorways and staying in the shadows, he was able to avoid most people. The ones he particularly wanted to avoid were the soldiers. He thought about going to see his shop and his employees to bid them farewell, but thought better of that. He also thought of trying to sneak in to see Catherine and tell her goodbye. But he thought better of that also, as it would put her in danger. No, the best course was for him is to try to escape alone.

In approaching the west gate, he saw many people coming and going. There were guards on the battlements of the gate and guards at the entrance. Some little shops were on the far side, away from gate, and a few of the shops had cooking pots. He made his way over to one of the shops and stealthily wiped smudge from the pots on his fingers. He rubbed the smudge onto his cheeks to camouflage his face and make it appear dirty from work. From this vantage point, he spied a group of workers walking toward the gate, apparently heading outside the city and going home from their day of work. He would try to blend in with them. As he approached the gate, he looked down and tried not to look at the guards. But just as he was about to pass through the gate, a guard yelled, "Halt!"

CHAPTER 24

Destiny

Captured once more by a very alert guard, John was thrown back roughly into the cell with the heretic, and the big, heavy door was slammed shut.

"How far did you get?" asked the heretic.

"I was passing through the gate. I almost made it," John said.

"It was not meant to be. We will die as martyrs, and that is how most prophets are treated."

With a tremble in his voice and apprehension is his eye, John said, "I'm scared! I'm afraid of the pain, and most of all, I'm afraid of the unknown after death. Is there no way out?" Then he began to cry.

The heretic got up from the floor, sat down next to John on his pallet of straw, and, facing him and holding his hands, said, "I, too, am afraid. But as prophets and martyrs, we must be an inspiration to force those cracks that will appear in the walls of ignorance and fear. Therefore, when it is our time, let us proceed with our heads held high. As to the unknown qualities of death, our bodies will return to the basic building blocks of physical existence. They will be recycled into new forms of life, a resurrection of sorts. Our spirit, our souls . . . whatever do those terms mean? They have never been adequately defined or conceptualized. Do they refer to our consciousness, personality, or maybe essence, whatever that is? Maybe we really don't have adequate human terms to define that essence. Whatever it is, it returns to and becomes part of the cosmos and God. And what that returning is like, only our deaths will answer."

He smiled gently at John. "So, my friend, there is a life after death, but it is not what has previously been imagined."

John gained some comfort from the heretic's words. It gave him much to think about, though little time to do it.

On the day prior to execution, a visitor arrived at the jail. The lock turned in John's cell, and the door opened. Instead of the guards, John saw Catherine.

"You have only five minutes, miss," the guard's voice growled.

"Catherine, Catherine, oh, God! How I missed you!" John exclaimed as they fell into each other's arms.

She said breathlessly, "John, I love you so. Are they treating you all right?"

He replied, "Yes, but I am so scared."

"I know darling, and so am I."

John asked, "Can your father to do something?"

"No, he has already tried. The archbishop will not give in."

"Then he must not try anymore," John said. "That will jeopardize his position and yours. And I cannot bear having you go through such trouble. Promise me that you will tell him not to do anymore."

Catherine nodded in defeat. John turned to the heretic and introduced him to Catherine. She nodded to the gentle man and received a smile in return.

"Your time is up," the guard announced as he came to the door. John and Catherine embraced one more time.

"I'll pray for you! I'll pray for you, my love," Catherine called as she was led away. John stood silent for several minutes, stunned. Then he collapsed against the wall, weeping.

The date of execution had arrived. John and the heretic were led out of the dungeon under heavy guard. As they were taken from the rear doors of the palace, low, dark clouds covered the city.

The two men, along with the student John had seen arrested at the university lecture hall, were put into a cart and were tied to a cross bar at the front of it. They were all wearing coarsely woven black wool tunics, which they had been given the night before. John was sweating with fear, and he felt the nausea of the condemned.

The prisoners were carted to the entrance of the basilica plaza, which was guarded by the fully armed palace Templars. A black pennant preceded the cart, the sign of execution and death. A priest followed, offering salvation for their repentance, but not their lives.

Crowds lined the streets, and drummers beat out a slow dirge as the prisoners were taken toward their place of execution. Some people were jeering and pelting the prisoners with stones and fruit. Others were pointing at the prisoners with expressions of sorrow, fear, or relief. John saw mothers and fathers whispering to their children and pointing.

After they arrived at the entrance to the basilica plaza, John and the others were taken off the cart, were bound together, and were marched through the crowd to a spot in front of the basilica, the place of execution. Three wooden stakes were erected on the cobblestone street at that spot. Brush, tree limbs, and other discarded wooden items were piled around the stakes. Soldiers from the sixth legion were stationed every five feet around the stakes to keep back the enormous crowd.

The prisoners were led up to the stakes and bound to them hand and foot. The heretic was placed in the center, the student on the left, and John on the right. A priest came out of the basilica and stood on the steps to read the decree in a measured canter, but John didn't follow the words at all. He was too busy searching the crowd for Catherine. His eyes finally found her as she sobbed in the crowd next to her father, who also was also weeping. His workers and the others John had come to know and love were also sobbing.

Louder than the sounds of their sobs were the voices of many citizens, who were shouting, "Heretic! Blasphemer!"

John was quite afraid. He found it harder and harder to breathe as his fear increased. He was trembling so much that he thought would shake apart, and his throat was so dry that he couldn't speak.

As the firewood was set alight, the heretic exclaimed, "Forgive them, forgive them, for they know not what they do!" The fire quickly covered him, and he was silent.

The student was screaming frantically, "Why? Why? Why?" He was struggling and wetting himself as the flames covered him.

At first, John noticed the smoke starting to come up from the wood. The smoke caused John to cough violently and to choke. Then gradually his feet and legs started to feel the flames. His tunic caught fire, and he could feel the piercing flames burning his skin. The pain grew more intense with every passing second. He screamed, "Oh, God! Oh, God, have mercy on me!" And then, blessedly, he passed out.

Then slowly, ever so slowly a sensation entered his being. His shoulder was being gently tapped and nudged. A voice, a familiar voice then started registering upon his mind, "John . . . John . . . Honey its time to get up. Its Sunday, you have a sermon to preach."